MYSTERIOUS SETTING

KAZUSHIGE ABE is one of Japan's pre-eminent contemporary writers. A graduate of the Japanese Institute of the Moving Image in Tokyo, he worked as an assistant director before turning his hand to writing. Since winning the Gunzo New Writers' Prize for his first novel, *Amerika no yoru*, he has been awarded several of Japan's most prestigious literary prizes, including the Sei Ito Award, the Mainichi Culture Award, the Akutagawa Prize and the Tanizaki Prize.

MICHAEL EMMERICH teaches Japanese literature at the University of California, Los Angeles. He is the translator of numerous books from Japanese by authors as diverse as Yasunari Kawabata, Yasushi Inoue, Gen'ichirō Takahashi, Banana Yoshimoto, and Hiromi Kawakami.

KAZUSHIGE ABE

MYSTERIOUS SETTING

Translated from the Japanese by

MICHAEL EMMERICH

PUSHKIN PRESS

Pushkin Press
Somerset House, Strand
London WC2R 1LA

English Translation rights arranged through CTB Inc.
English translation by Michael Emmerich

First published in Japan with the title *Mysterious
Setting* by The Asahi Shimbun Company.

First published by Pushkin Press in 2024

1 3 5 7 9 8 6 4 2

ISBN 13: 978-1-80533-048-6

Designed and typeset by Tetragon, London

Printed and bound in the United Kingdom by Clays Ltd, Elcograf S.p.A.

www.pushkinpress.com

MYSTERIOUS SETTING

MYSTERIOUS SETTING

A sophisticated jewelry-making technique in which princess-cut jewels are set without the gold or platinum prongs that typically hold stones in place, allowing their inherent beauty to shine forth to the fullest extent. Pioneered by Van Cleef & Arpels, the technique is officially known as the "Mystery Set."

ARAB NEWSPAPER SAYS AL-QAEDA BOUGHT NUCLEAR WEAPONS FROM UKRAINE IN 1998

CAIRO (Reuters) – The pan-Arab newspaper *Al-Hayat* reported on February 8 that in 1998 al-Qaeda, the international terrorist network headed by Osama bin Laden, purchased suitcases outfitted with tactical nuclear weapons from Ukraine, and that the organization is holding them for possible detonation in the United States or other countries. [...] Ukraine inherited a nuclear arsenal from the Soviet Union on achieving independence in 1991, but in 1994 it agreed to send 1,900 warheads to Russia and sign on to the Nuclear Non-Proliferation Treaty.

The Asahi Shimbun, February 9, 2004

WHERE ARE THE SUITCASE NUKES NOW?

In September 1997, former Russian National Security Advisor Alexander Lebed testified that of the 132 suitcase-sized nuclear bombs once in Russia's possession, all but 48 remained unaccounted for. Although the Russian government denies having developed such devices, a scientist who served as advisor to President Yeltsin has confirmed their existence, and the United States believes that Russia still maintains an arsenal of compact nuclear weapons. In recent years, witnesses have testified that Osama bin Laden may have acquired approximately twenty suitcase nukes from Chechen militants. The bombs measure 60 x 40 x 20 centimeters, making them roughly as portable as ordinary suitcases.

THERE WAS A PERIOD, a long time ago now, when I used to go play in this park a lot with my friends. I suppose I must have been about ten or so.

I call it a park, but really it was just a field—no slide, no swings, no jungle gym.

There were these long rows of old stones, chipped and crumbling, like markers of some sort, but that was it. Large stones, small stones. Wherever you looked, that's all there was.

The park was neither attractive nor nice, but it was quite spacious. Actually, it was *huge*. My friends and I had more space there than we could ever need.

The park was kind of far away—it took over an hour to bike there from where we lived—but we liked making the trip together, and we went all the time.

Basically, we had nowhere else to play.

There were five or six kids in the group I hung out with, so we couldn't stay indoors for long. We lived in pretty small houses, and our parents were constantly getting after us. We were too poor to afford any sort of entertainment we had to pay for.

So we would head out to that wide-open park where we could horse around as much as we wanted without worrying that anyone would complain. To that vast field of rubble.

And what did we do when we got there?

We listened to the old man.

When we first discovered the park, we used to play chicken on our bikes or jump from one crumbling block to the next, eager to prove how brave we were. All that stopped when we met the old man. From then on, we just went and listened to him talk.

His stories weren't that interesting—they were kind of boring, actually. Something in the way he told them really drew us in, though, leaving us all mesmerized.

I don't know, maybe we were just desperate for something to do. Anything, it didn't matter what. It still amazes me, though, looking back, that we stuck with him as long as we did. That we never tired of the old guy and his silly tales.

There was something in the air, I think. Some peculiar feeling you couldn't quite put your finger on that kept calling us back, over and over. Yes, the park was like that. It had a special magnetism that drew you in and held you—that wouldn't let you go.

Why else would kids hungry for action have biked so far to such a desolate place?

And we weren't the only ones. The park was surprisingly crowded, full of people doing the kinds of things you do in a park. Housewives walking dogs, couples lounging under the trees, old men playing *shōgi*, young men who had stripped off their shirts to sunbathe. High-school girls practicing dance moves, boys kicking soccer balls around. It was all perfectly ordinary—everything except the park itself, which seemed too dreary to be so popular. Or rather, it felt odd that it was so popular, given how dreary it was.

That's why I say there must have been something special about it.

Something that called us all there, irresistibly.

To that park.

●

I've forgotten the old man's stories. All that has stayed with me is the sense that, by and large, they were pretty dull. I don't regret having forgotten them, not really, though there is a certain frustration in being unable to remember.

One thing I do remember quite clearly is how we met the man.

Given how crowded the park was, no one would have looked out of place. There were people who came up and tried to sell you stuff, and just wouldn't let you alone; a priest who was there every day, intoning his eerie spells; a steady stream of officials and researchers who claimed to be working on environmental surveys; scientists conducting obscure experiments with outlandish equipment. Every so often, a group of volunteers came to plant trees.

I figure it was those crowds of people who gathered in the park to enjoy themselves that brought the old man there. He needed the human contact. None of us ever went with him to his house, but we got the impression he lived alone.

And it wasn't as if he just swung by the park in the course of his daily walk. He was there on a mission. Not like he had some goal he was trying to accomplish—that's not the sort of mission I mean. It was about trying to help the people around him. He was engaged in a very private sort of volunteer work. He performed for the children in the park.

Kamishibai, as it's called. Paper theater.

That, at least, was his plan. The world, however, planted an obstacle in his path. No one paid any attention to the shows he staged in his little corner of that vast park, showing hand-drawn pictures as he narrated the story they depicted. No one, young or old, had any desire to experience such an old-fashioned entertainment.

I can't tell you how long he kept up those sad performances.

Over time, though, even as the park's visitors kept ignoring him, they must have begun to notice his presence, as he stood there in the same spot day after day, rotating through the series of pictures and recounting his stories to a non-existent audience.

One day, one of the boys in my group suggested we go tease him. You can imagine it, I'm sure—a bunch of ten-year-olds going to harass an old man and becoming friendly with him instead. That was how we ended up opening the gate to his invisible amphitheater.

I see only one possible explanation for our subsequent transformation, as we morphed from a gaggle of hecklers into a well-behaved audience.

That same magnetism.

As I said, the stories themselves were so boring that it was only natural no one ever came to watch, and the old man had none of the charm or charisma that makes certain people so irresistibly fascinating to others. Could this very lack of charisma have been the thing that drew us back? Maybe we were just being nice?

No, I don't think so. None of us was so generous, and, besides, I wouldn't say we felt sorry for him. Certainly, I don't recall ever feeling that way. He had a sense of purpose, after all, and he didn't seem particularly lonely.

Eventually, after we began meeting the old man on a regular basis and had even spoken with him a few times, he told us about himself. He was a teacher, he said. One of us asked what school he taught at, and he said he didn't really work any-more—he was retired. He still thought of himself as a teacher, though, even if he no longer had a classroom. That was why he came each day to perform at the park: telling stories was a form of instruction. Finding students had proved to be more difficult than he expected, but he didn't let that trouble him; he kept at it, offering his free classes to the public.

That's the sort of man he was. And it's true, there was something vaguely classroom-like in our interactions with him. At least that's how it seems in retrospect. Not that we disliked him, as we did some of our teachers at school—though here, too, it may have been that some of the park's special magnetism had rubbed off on him.

I said I've forgotten the old man's stories, but actually there is one that I remember very clearly. One of the stories he told will stay with me forever.

It's the reason I can still recall the old man so vividly.

Which is exactly how he wanted it.

He was determined that we should hold on to that story no matter what might happen to us in our lives, however many years passed. He told us so himself many times, so often it got annoying. All he wanted was for us to remember that story—it was the whole reason he had gone on teaching past his retirement.

The story wasn't wildly funny, or even amusing. There was no soaring fantasy, and it didn't have any sort of cathartic effect. The plot had its share of ups and downs, I suppose, but I can't imagine anyone really enjoying it.

What else can I say? And say with confidence?

That everyone who heard it felt a little sad, I guess.

Maybe "everyone" is going too far.

But if there were five or six people listening, at least one or two would be touched.

And so they would remember the story, and then eventually the day would come when they would feel the urge to pass the story on to someone else.

Now that the old man had found his students, he quit *kamishibai*. We were good enough listeners, he said, that he could do without the pictures. The story was better without them, because he could really get into the details.

From then on, when he called us over to his little corner of the park, he would just plop himself down on the soft earth and lean against the fence. And the performance would begin.

He started each story with the same set phrase. *Every tale has one or two main characters*, he would declaim, *and of course the one I'm about to tell you is no exception.*

This was how the story began.

And it continued...

●

I'm going to call the protagonist of this story Shiori.

Shiori moved to Tokyo at eighteen; it seems she was originally from Tōhoku Region.

We're talking ancient history, here—back when I was in my teens.

Shiori doesn't seem to have had a very happy life. Fate wasn't really on her side. But she was an optimist, and seldom let things get her down. More importantly, she had a dream. She had come to Tokyo to become a lyricist.

Shiori never gave up, no matter what happened. That's the kind of person she was. She could tolerate any sort of agony, physical or mental, as long as she was able to keep believing that enduring it would help her realize her dream. She couldn't escape the pain outright, but she could numb it by picturing herself sometime in the future, hard at work on a song. She wasn't actually writing any lyrics right now, but still she could imagine herself—a sparkling, glamorous version of herself—deeply engrossed in conversation with the singers she would eventually get to know. That vision was always with her, a high-resolution image tucked away in the recesses of her mind.

She had decided to become a lyricist because she was tone deaf.

Yes, Shiori was tone deaf. And yet she loved music, so that from the time she was young, whenever a song touched her she would start singing along.

People always got annoyed when she did this, so she tried to sing as softly as she could. As a child, she thought the volume was the problem.

In any event, Shiori was constantly singing. And so she knew, she just *knew*, that she was destined to live with music.

She asked her mother about this once, and her mother agreed she might be right. When she became pregnant, Shiori's mother had gone to stay with her parents so they could look after her, and she had spent a lot of time playing their piano. She hoped it would serve as a sort of prenatal training, but since she had never taken piano lessons and couldn't read music, few of the chords she produced were beautiful or harmonious. Shiori's aunt had grown up playing that piano, not Shiori's mother.

Later on, Shiori would come to the conclusion that she owed her tone deafness to that awful piano playing of her mother's, but she never felt any resentment.

Soon after she started middle school, Shiori learned the word *troubadour*. She was flipping through a book at the library when it caught her eye.

She didn't much like to read, and she hadn't entirely grasped what the word meant when she put the book down, but just seeing it on the page and repeating it in her head made her feel all tingly inside. The moment she got home, she dashed up to her room and started a troubadour notebook. It wasn't for poems, however; it was for pictures. She covered page after page with drawings of troubadours as she saw them in her fantasies—figures that grew more and more wondrous, less and less human. She wasn't very good at drawing, either.

From that day on, Shiori knew she would live as a troubadour. The next time she sat down with her teacher for guidance counseling, she announced that she had made up her mind not to continue on to high school. There was no need, she said, because she was a troubadour. There was a phone call home and her mother had to come in for a talk, but Shiori didn't get in trouble just yet. Her mother thought it was a terrific idea. Her father gave her a thorough scolding, though, and in the end she went to high school after all.

The troubadour suffered a good deal of persecution.

In middle school she had been the subject of numerous "witch hunts" by her classmates, to which she had responded by making sure never to sing in anyone else's presence—and when the storm came, simply waiting for it to blow over.

Things weren't as bad in high school, though a few unfortunate experiences revealed to her the awesome the power of music.

The worst was when, three times in a fairly short period, she allowed herself to sing very softly at school—and on each occasion a fellow student had died the next day. One was killed in a car crash; one committed suicide; the third was stabbed by a boy from another school. All three students were girls.

Shiori couldn't begin to imagine how her singing might be linked to these tragedies, but the connection terrified her all the same. She felt a profound sense of guilt, and now she was more careful than ever not to sing in public.

Even before the three deaths, those middle-school witch hunts had taught Shiori that she needed to keep her troubadour identity hidden from her high-school classmates. Whenever possible, she would beg off singing in music class or in the karaoke booth, and, if she couldn't refuse outright, she would feign shyness, singing so faintly that no one could hear.

Still, whenever something moved her deeply, the song would come. Her voice would burst forth all on its own, revealing her troubadour nature. Everyone, from her closest friends to random students she hardly knew, would freeze, stunned, their faces registering disgust.

Each time this happened, Shiori would remember something her social studies teacher had told her in middle school.

All poets are alone.

It made Shiori sad to think that poets, even singing poets, were so shunned and isolated. Though this also explained why they spent so much time alone with their verses.

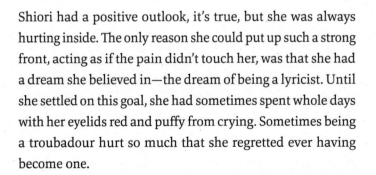

Shiori had a positive outlook, it's true, but she was always hurting inside. The only reason she could put up such a strong front, acting as if the pain didn't touch her, was that she had a dream she believed in—the dream of being a lyricist. Until she settled on this goal, she had sometimes spent whole days with her eyelids red and puffy from crying. Sometimes being a troubadour hurt so much that she regretted ever having become one.

She never gave up on her musical life, though. One thing she did to keep the dream alive was to stop at a pet shop on her way home from school.

This shop occupied part of the ground floor of a large supermarket Shiori had passed on her way to middle school, and still passed going to high school now. Her family had two cats, and they had been shopping here for ages. At first, she used to swing by on her way home to get supplies for the cats, on whom she doted: kitty litter, toys, cat food. Often, she bought more than was necessary, and sometimes more than she could even carry, so she had to have the items delivered, and her father would scold her for wasting money.

Shiori's mother had the same habit. Whenever she had a spare moment, she would drive the family car to the store and stockpile cat goods. It got to the point where her husband felt he had to tell her to stop. Frequently they had so much stuff at home that they could have set up shop themselves. Shiori's mother didn't see this as a problem, though, and Shiori learned from her example, visiting the pet shop whenever the spirit moved her to see what new products had come in.

I'm a slave to our cats, she sometimes thought.

Then, on one of her many visits, the slave found a new master.

Or rather, masters. The store had lots of them. They lived in cages, and had colorful wings, and twittered adorably. Shiori had seen parakeets in the past, of course, but she had never looked at them in this way before. She began to feel that no form of life was more perfect than these birds.

Unsurprisingly, it was song that brought Shiori and the parakeets together, though she hadn't really intended to sing to them. She always came to the store alone, but just because there was no one around to hear her didn't mean she was free to do whatever she wanted.

The parakeets' tweeting had been part of the store's atmosphere from the start, of course, but the background music, the sounds of people talking, and all the other noise had kept her from paying much attention. Then one day, just like that, she realized that the birds weren't just tweeting, they were *singing,* and from that moment her heart was theirs.

How did this happen, you ask? What made her realize that the parakeets were, in fact, singing? She learned, purely by chance, from a stranger.

Shiori had been holding a pair of tiny cat bells to her ear, gently swaying them back and forth so she could enjoy their tinkle, calming her wounded troubadour heart, when all of a sudden, over in the bird section, someone started shouting.

"Sing! George! Please, please sing! Sing for me!"

Turning toward the voice, Shiori saw a woman about her mother's age pleading with one of the parakeets. She was dressed in a Tyrolean costume.

"Please, George! I beg you! Sing for me, sing again!..."

The woman's voice was full of passion. The next moment, she seized the cage and began rattling it. A clerk ran over, abandoning a customer at the register.

"Excuse me! Excuse me! Please don't do that!"

Unmoved by the clerk's intervention, the Tyrolean-costumed woman kept pleading with the bird. "Yes, yes! Sing more, George! Sing for me, keep singing!"

Her plaintive cries could be heard for some time even after the guard led her out, dragging her from behind by the arms. It felt almost as if the woman herself had been singing, her voice transforming a section of the supermarket into a concert hall.

That, at any rate, was how Shiori felt. For a few minutes, she stood motionless and dazed, blocking out all information from the outside world. The supermarket was full of shoppers and clerks, an incredible profusion of objects, but for a few minutes Shiori felt as though her body were suspended in a pure white space, a vacuum.

Only the parakeets' faint singing reached her.

"Ah," she thought. Then, for no reason, "George!"

Suddenly gripped by a desire to move, she hurried to the cages. For the first time, she genuinely *listened* to the parakeets' singing. Their voices enveloped her, drew her in deeper and deeper, until, without even realizing it, she too had begun to sing—right there in the middle of the store, her voice merging with theirs.

Clerks and shoppers turned to look, regarding her with

the same revulsion she had seen so many times before on the faces of her friends and classmates. None of them was happy to hear her singing, she could see that. But the parakeets in their wire cages reacted completely differently.

All at once, the birds, even those that had remained silent until then, raised their voices in a magnificent chorus of twittering. They were pleased that Shiori had been moved to join their song.

The noise was so deafening that everyone nearby had to cover their ears. Shiori glanced around, shaken, then turned back to the cage. There was a new liveliness in the parakeets' eyes, and she could see that they were trying to say something to her as they warbled at the top of their lungs—to communicate some message.

They're welcoming me.

It was true. She could sense it. The birds were singing their joy, together, telling her how happy they were that she had joined them. That's what this outburst meant. That, at any rate, was how Shiori interpreted it. That was what she heard in their trilling.

Please, Shiori! Sing more! Keep singing for us, we beg you!

She was profoundly moved. Of course she was! In all her life, no one had ever responded with such passion to her singing. She was so touched that she burst into tears.

"I'm sorry, but I can't—it might disturb the other shoppers. I'm so sorry, really. But I'll come again, OK? I'll come visit you, I just won't sing. If I did, they'd drag me off like that woman earlier, and then we'd never see each other again. Well, maybe occasionally, when no one else is around—maybe I could sing very softly. So please don't be angry with me for not singing now. And thank you, all of you! You've made me so happy, speaking so kindly about my singing."

One of the clerks was eyeing her. He didn't care how much she spent, he wasn't going to have her making grotesque noises in the shop, hurting business. That, at any rate, was how Shiori read his expression. And so, having quietly communicated her gratitude to the parakeets, she left the store for the day.

Now she had a new reason to visit the pet shop.

Indeed, over time, shopping for the cats became little more than an excuse. Her hushed conversations with the parakeets were much more important. The joyful, welcoming song they launched into each time they saw Shiori was a source of strength and encouragement.

Naturally, she begged her parents to let her have some as pets.

Her mother refused. If you've got cats, she said, you can't have birds.

She had a point, Shiori admitted, but she kept pushing even so. It would be fine, she said, she'd just have to make sure the birds never got out of her room.

And who, her mother replied, will look after them when you go out? Shiori had no reply. She hadn't thought things through that carefully.

Her mother's disapproval was a serious blow. Her father opposed the plan for the same reasons, so in the end Shiori had to abandon her vision of a life with parakeets.

In the end, her mother was probably right. The birds would be happier with their friends at the store, rather than living in constant fear of a cat attack. Even Shiori could understand that, now that she had given up on her plan.

The longer the birds remained together, the more joyful their lives would be. They were happiest in each other's company, even if it was only a matter of time until they were carted off, one by one, to become someone's pet.

Shiori felt terribly sad, once again, when she realized this. No other poet was as lonely as she was. Her younger sister, Nozomi, came to say that dinner was ready, but Shiori just said she wasn't hungry and stayed in her room, sobbing uncontrollably.

●

To a large extent, Shiori owed her thick skin to her sister.

You don't develop such resilience in a day or two, of course. Little by little, over many years, her heart had been steeled until almost nothing could dent it.

Strength of that sort can't be measured, and since Shiori had never been one to compare herself to others in this regard it was hard to gauge just how thick-skinned she had become. Still, it was certainly impressive how much more mature she was now, in high school, than she had been back in elementary school, when she cried every day. These days she cried no more than two or three times a week.

Though it was true Nozomi had toughened Shiori up, she was also the reason Shiori had become such a crybaby in the first place.

Nozomi showed no restraint in talking to Shiori. She was a sharp-tongued, pitiless girl who said exactly what she thought. And she had never looked up to her older sister—perhaps because they were born in the same year. If anything, Shiori tended to behave with a certain deference toward Nozomi. Their relationship had been that way ever since they were babies.

So, of course, Nozomi made no attempt to comfort Shiori that evening.

"What's got into you, wanting parakeets all of a sudden?" Nozomi asked.

Shiori made the mistake of answering truthfully. She knew her sister was the last person she should tell about the amazing occurrence at the pet store, but she couldn't help it. She was exhausted from crying and wasn't thinking straight.

"How do know they liked your singing?" Nozomi asked when she finished.

Shiori recounted how the birds had burst into song.

"What was their singing like?"

Without going overboard, Shiori briefly imitated their cries. *Gyaa! Gyaa!*

"*That's* how they sounded? If you ask me, I think they must have been irritated. And they were *all* making that noise? Honestly, Shiori, I don't think they meant to be welcoming—just the opposite. They were pleading with you to stop."

Such was the harsh judgment Nozomi handed down.

Shiori promptly submitted her appeal. It only seemed that way, she suggested, because she had done such a bad imitation of their cries. For a second time, she transformed herself into a cage of parakeets, drawing a deeper breath than before and striving to get the tone just right.

Gyaa-aa! Gyaa-aa!

"Shiori, enough! Shriek all you like, it won't change anything. It's beyond me how you could interpret that as anything other than an expression of displeasure. I'm sure you were just misreading the signs, like you always do. The parakeets were begging you to stop, and somehow you got it into your head that it was a song of joy. It's always like that with you, isn't it? You really need to fix that. It's high time you stopped being so self-centered."

Shiori almost burst out crying again, but she fought the tears back.

Nozomi eyed her older sister, who sat with her face screwed up, hanging her head. Nozomi herself was beaming, her cheeks pinching her eyes. This cheerful expression did not signal, however, that Nozomi was ready to relent. She seemed instead to have decided that this was the moment for a swift second attack.

"Listen, Shiori. Dragging animals into your own human fantasies is one of the dumbest things a person can do. Everyone knows that. Do you have even the slightest familiarity with parakeets? How could you possibly think you understand their cries? What arrogance! Oh, sure, it's nice for you, feeling like you've been validated or whatever, but just put yourself in the place of those poor birds! I'll never be able to show my face in the pet shop again—not after you've inflicted such pain on those helpless darlings. It's inconceivable, really. Persuading yourself they're thrilled to see you, then talking to them—not just talking, actually *singing* at them... Just picturing it gives me goosebumps. Look at me, I'm shivering. And you're so completely oblivious you don't even notice the damage you're doing! It's more than I can take, honestly. I'm ashamed to be related to you."

Tears welled in Shiori's eyes as she stared at her sister.

"Maybe I misunderstood the parakeets," she said, her voice quivering, "and if I did that was wrong of me, and I should learn from my mistake. But I never forced them to do anything, and I only sang three times."

"You wanted to bring some home as pets, right? When you have a pet, nine times out of ten you start treating them like they're your playthings. I can totally see it now—just look how you treat our cats! You'd start buying all kinds of crap, filling the cage with pointless gewgaws, and, before you know it, you'd have a bunch of hyperstressed birds on your hands."

Shiori denied having any such intentions. She thought the birds would be comforting, that was all—seeing them every day, listening to them sing. Was that wrong, too?

"What do you think? Listen, Shiori. I want you to use your brain for a little, OK? Before you started going on about getting those parakeets, did you ever pause to consider what it would be like to have them here, given the nature of Dad's work?"

This was a somewhat malicious question. Their father ran a *yakitori* chain with locations throughout the southern Tōhoku Region.

Was it wrong, Shiori stammered, for a family to keep pet birds just because its members fed and clothed themselves by selling chunks of chicken on skewers?

This only made things worse.

"No, it isn't *wrong*. That's not what I'm saying. I'm just trying to understand your attitude, that's all. I mean, your own family lives by slaughtering birds, right? Day after day, we send thousands, tens of thousands of birds to their deaths, and you want your cute little darlings in the pet store to come and 'comfort' you. Talk about a split personality! Whatever, as long as it suits your needs, right? If you ask me, you rely way too much on these poor birds. I'm trying to work out how you manage the cognitive dissonance. That's the point that interests me. It's perfectly fine to turn living creatures into tools, I guess, if it makes your life easier? Is that how you see it? Like, in your mind the birds are no different from your cell phone?"

"No," Shiori grumbled, "that's not what I think."

She hadn't meant to grumble, but her voice was in retreat. Nozomi's needling had made her mouth go dry, and she was hoarse.

"Then what *were* you thinking? What inspired you to ask if you could have those parakeets as pets? What do they mean to you?"

"I love them, I think they're wonderful!" she said. "I wish I could be one!"

With this, the dam broke. She started wailing.

Those sobs... There was something delicious in the rhythm of her gasping, a beauty every bit as beguiling as her singing was unpleasant. And the longer Shiori wept, the more alluring the sound became. Everyone who heard it felt better, as if all were right with the world.

Despite the haughty disdain she felt for her sister, Nozomi was no different. Indeed, ever since they were both young, Nozomi had taken every opportunity to reduce her sister to tears, simply so she could hear those wondrous cries. She was in love with Shiori's tears.

Now that she had accomplished her goal, Nozomi sat gazing raptly at her bawling sister, a smile playing across her lips that suggested not merely satisfaction, but ecstasy. She watched her, and kept watching, and then watched some more.

Under the observant eye of her nosey sister—a young woman who periodically assumed the mien of a police officer or a judge—Shiori was unable to bring her sobbing under control. She wailed and wailed. And then she wailed some more.

●

Nozomi scolded Shiori for all sorts of reasons, but Shiori didn't really listen.

Each time Nozomi cornered her like this, she would try to offer a proper rebuttal, but she could never find the right words, and she lost every debate.

When Shiori burst out crying at the end of these exchanges, it wasn't a sudden welling-up of frustration, or hurt, or sadness, or even anger at her own incompetence that prompted her tears. It was all these things together.

Nozomi had always bullied her this way, so Shiori was used to it. By now she could more or less foresee the trajectory an exchange would take. But knowing the scenario Nozomi had in mind didn't help: Shiori was still incapable of holding her own. Initially, she would keep calm as Nozomi fired question after question at her, appraising the situation objectively and warning herself not to be deceived, because this was what always happened; but sooner or later Nozomi always found some way to get her worked up and make her cry.

Shiori half-thought Nozomi must be taking lessons in hypnosis. She couldn't understand how her sister could reduce her to tears so often, even though it was perfectly obvious that's what she was trying to do, unless she was exploiting some special technique.

Despite everything, though, the sisters didn't dislike each other. Nozomi made Shiori cry, but they weren't on bad terms. They harbored no deep mutual animosity; indeed, they were the sort of siblings who could share any secret.

At least superficially, then, there was no rift between them. This despite the considerable differences in their personalities, of which Shiori herself was aware. In fact, you could have divided their family right down the middle by personality type: Shiori and her mother were romantics; Nozomi and her father were realists.

Not surprisingly, seeing as they lived under the same roof, Shiori and Nozomi had plenty of opportunities to disagree. And every time they did, Shiori ended up crying.

Nozomi knew Shiori considered herself a troubadour, of course. They had talked about it when Shiori was in her third year of middle school, on the same day Shiori stunned her teacher by announcing that she didn't want to go to high school.

"What does that mean, Shiori? What does a troubadour do?"

A troubadour, Shiori explained, traveled the land, composing and singing poems.

"Then how could you possibly be one? I mean, you don't travel, and you can't write poems. If that's what a troubadour is, then you aren't a troubadour."

Shiori was used to fending off Nozomi's negativity.

It's true, she said, she wasn't a traveler yet, but she was planning to run away from home after she finished middle school. And while she hadn't written her poems down, she had lots that she could share at any time, as long as it was OK for her to sing them.

Nozomi asked why, if she was prepared to share her poems, she didn't write them down.

This was a good question, and Shiori was unsure how to answer. She didn't know why.

Nozomi was merciless at moments like this.

"Things just spin further out of control when you try to cover up one lie with another, Shiori. Why not admit you can't write poetry? You'd like to be a poet, but you aren't one, and, if you ask me, the odds you'll succeed in becoming a 'troubadour' seem pretty slim. They say everyone has the right to dream, but inflicting a 'right' like that on people seems cruel to me. Just look at you, shooting off lies so transparent even I can see through them, acting like this dumb 'dream' of yours is your greatest treasure and you'll never let it go. I've never heard anything so stupid in my life."

Shiori couldn't let these brutal criticisms pass. She would prove she was a troubadour by performing one of her poems. And so, without warning, she sprang to her feet and burst into song. She held nothing back, giving full vent to her emotions.

There's no way to represent her poem in language. Because she herself didn't use words; it was all in the modulation of her voice. There was nothing unusual in this, as far as she was concerned. At that point in her life, she often created songs using whatever random sounds felt right to her in the moment.

Unfortunately, Nozomi was not persuaded. On the contrary, she rejected Shiori's singing. She became genuinely incensed. Her assessment was so harsh it bordered on abuse.

"What the fuck was that? There must be something wrong with you, Shiori. My god, I thought my ears were going to split! You think anyone would even recognize that as singing? Give me a break. And I don't just mean people today, who are alive right now. I'm talking about the whole history of the human race. You could go back to the Middle Ages, or the Stone Age, or jump forward a century from now—no one would call that singing. And you're telling me that's not just a song, but a *poem*? There wasn't a single recognizable word! Please don't tell me it was your enunciation—I couldn't take that. If no one can make sense of it, it isn't a word. Or were you *trying* to be unintelligible? Listen, Shiori, you don't have to get all aggressive just because you can't write a proper poem—that won't soften the pain. People lash out like that when they're desperate. Please never do that in my presence again—no more moaning like that, like an *animal*. Don't do it in front of *anyone.* Please. You'll make people sick. They'll get nauseous. Noise like that would make a baby vomit, I swear. Thank goodness there were no babies here! Honestly, my stomach was churning, and I'm not even a baby."

Shiori felt something churning inside her, too. Not the contents of her stomach, though. It was pain. Her vision blurred, as if she were seeing the world through wet goggles, and she just stood there sniveling.

Still, she couldn't give in without a fight.

Maybe she would never convince Nozomi she was a troubadour, even if she spent years trying. But she couldn't let herself be defeated so easily, accepting Nozomi's unalloyed rejection and wallowing in her sorrow. She knew she wasn't entirely wrong to say she was a troubadour. From her perspective, she would be lying if she agreed with Nozomi, and not the other way around.

This time, she tried to explain using words others could understand.

That's how I sing, she declared nasally, and that's what my poems are like. Singing that way feels right to me, and it feels the most natural, she went on, choosing her words with care. There are no lies in my songs; they express my emotions just as they are.

Shiori felt a small sense of accomplishment as she finished. She had been quite articulate, she thought, at least by her standards.

But the debate wasn't over.

"Well then, you should stop singing. If that unintelligible groaning is what you call poetry, and if that's the kind of singing that feels right to you, then you should just keep quiet. If those noises have no meaning, you haven't said anything. Keeping your mouth shut also has the advantage of not making everyone around you feel nasty. Listen to me, Shiori. The world is noisy enough—we don't need you adding to the racket. All right? I've done my duty as your sister. I've warned you. If you decide to keep singing anyway, even after all I've said, then you'll be doing wrong *knowingly*. You'll be committing a crime of sorts. And I'll have no choice but to punish you. This is extremely important, Shiori. As your sister, as the one person who understands you better than anyone else, that's my responsibility."

Evidently Nozomi had appointed herself Shiori's judge. Seeing the stern look on her face, Shiori got the sense that even a bit of humming would be met with a punishment so severe it would seem entirely disproportionate to the offense.

Shiori was shaken.

Nozomi was always dictatorial, but it hurt to be told that her that singing was a crime.

Shiori could sort of see where Nozomi was coming from. In middle school, it had been her singing that triggered the "witch hunts," and when she considered how people had reacted to her music over the years, she had to admit it wasn't exactly popular with the masses.

Nozomi had made her see this. Shiori felt its truth, and she was stunned.

She was still sitting there in silence, crushed by the weight of the decision she had to make, when her sister spoke again, determined to strike one final blow.

"Are you afraid of being punished? Is that why you're just sitting there? Well, if that fear prevents you from singing, then you won't be hurting anyone, and that will be a step in the right direction. I assume you're over that ludicrous notion of skipping high school, too—that'll be a relief for your teacher. I have to say, though, you sure are a pushover, Shiori. You can't have cared much about becoming a troubadour, seeing as it was so easy for you to give it up. I guess the whole thing was just a silly, pointless whim. That's how it is with dreams, right? They're insubstantial, empty."

Devastated as she was, this grated on Shiori's nerves. She almost never got angry, but this time she couldn't help it—not when her deep determination to live as a troubadour had been dismissed as a passing whim.

When Shiori was overcome by a powerful emotion, she would usually vent by singing, weaving her feelings into an impromptu poem. Now wasn't really the time for that. Instead, like the subjects of a brutal regime suddenly inspired by a hunger for freedom, she kindled her fighting spirit. She took a deep breath and told Nozomi firmly that she was mistaken. Shiori's being a troubadour, her singing, wasn't pointless at all.

"Yes, yes. Obviously you would want to believe that, wouldn't you? But tell me something, Shiori: have you ever made any effort to persuade others of that? I heard you sing just now, and it meant absolutely nothing to me. And why is that? Because you aren't even *trying* to make yourself understood, that's why. That's the issue. It's not the meaninglessness of what you're doing that makes it a crime—it's that you insist it *is* meaningful without attempting to shape that meaning into words. And then you jump all over anyone who doubts you, saying it's about giving voice to your feelings, that's all that matters. *That's* your sin. It's irresponsible."

Nozomi seemed determined to cut Shiori down.

Shiori, meanwhile, refused to be cowed.

"You may be right," she said, "but my singing still has meaning."

"Then now is the time for you to explain it. If you can't, we'll never get anywhere, no matter how long we go on like this. Will you do that for me? Help me see what your poems are about, in words I can understand. What are you singing? What earthly reason do you have for wanting to be a troubadour, of all things?"

Shiori could answer this easily.

"There are moments when I feel very clearly that I'm part of the natural world, and I give voice to this feeling by singing whatever bubbles up in my heart, just as it comes. The more I sing, the more the line between me and nature blurs. That's why I want to travel the world, and live my life as a troubadour."

Shiori thought this was pretty good, but Nozomi wasn't satisfied.

"If that's what your poems are about, they're pathetically empty. I shouldn't have bothered. What a waste of time. Whatever, it doesn't matter. Basically, you just want to sing for yourself. You're a typical self-absorbed, self-satisfied narcissist."

"No, I'm not!" Shiori muttered without thinking.

"What do you mean, 'No I'm not!'? Are you're telling me you're *not* self-absorbed and self-satisfied? Trust me, Shiori, that's exactly what you are. When you go around believing you're singing, when you're just howling at random, that's the only conclusion that can be drawn. You aren't helping anyone with that; you're just pleasing yourself."

Tears welled in Shiori's eyes. Once again, she said it wasn't true. Then, lured on by her sister's words, or by some spirit in the air, she began describing the future she envisioned for herself as a troubadour.

She had never thought the plan through, and it was a bit outrageous.

As she wandered the earth, she would come into contact with various plants and flowers, and she would spin her intuitive appreciation of the ideas present in nature itself into poetry, making herself nature's voice—and, as a result, ecosystems would be kept in proper balance, and countless people and animals would be saved. Maybe, she added, she was set on living as a troubadour because she hoped that one day, through her singing, she would dissolve completely into nature, and then she could watch over the people of the world as they lived their lives in peace.

All this came out with surprising ease.

"Shiori, that's absurd. Seriously, only an idiot could fantasize about something so dumb. Let's just stop here, OK? You'll only get weirder if we continue."

And so Nozomi gave up and drew the curtain on their debate.

Having the discussion cut off in this way upset Shiori. Nozomi had effectively dismissed the whole future Shiori imagined for herself, and this hurt and saddened her.

●

Things were easy for Nozomi. It was like being allowed to go second in a game of rock-paper-scissors: she simply had to object to everything Shiori said, finding a way to trip her up with each new turn the conversation took. The finest hair-splitting had the effect of truth.

Nozomi's consistent negativity made everything Shiori said sound like an excuse. To make matters worse, her cross-examining confused Shiori, sending her scampering, first one way, then another, until finally there was nowhere left for her to go, neither forward nor backward. And then, when they had talked past each other sufficiently, gone as far as they could on parallel tracks, Shiori would burst into tears. That was the pattern.

A stranger, seeing the two sisters argue, would have assumed they hated each other, but their parents and their friends understood that all this quarreling was just a game—a secret sport only they knew how to play.

For a while, their parents had intervened whenever they saw the two arguing, but the girls never reformed their ways. Again and again, the parents had reminded Shiori that she was the big sister, she shouldn't be such a crybaby; and they had told Nozomi to try to make Shiori feel more like she was the elder one. None of this had any effect. Nothing the parents said mattered. The girls were completely absorbed in the game, and as soon as conditions were favorable they would launch right into another unmistakably lopsided contest.

In any event, the sisters didn't always argue. Usually they got along.

This puzzled their parents. Why did they argue if they were so close? Eventually, though, they grew accustomed to the situation, and it no longer seemed like a big deal.

The sisters kept at it, time after time, going back and forth in their game-like fashion, and their parents stopped interfering. The girls never fought physically, after all, and their quarrels didn't appear to be pushing them apart. There was probably no reason to worry.

At any rate, that was the conclusion they reached. They encouraged each other with the convenient cliché that arguments were a sign of intimacy, and gradually persuaded themselves it was true.

But what about Shiori's tears?

There was a touch of hypocrisy in her parents' injunction that she stop crying all the time and act like a big sister. Sometimes they scolded her when they were out of the house, saying her wailing embarrassed them, only to let her wail as loudly as she liked when they were at home. Often they simply sat and watched her cry. Even when they offered words of sympathy or comfort, their faces remained oddly bright, as if her sobbing meant no more to them than the chirping of a cricket.

Perhaps somewhere in their hearts they felt the same way Nozomi did. Maybe they, too, were bewitched by the music of her sobs.

And so Nozomi grew more brazen. Something in the air at home signaled to her that she was free to do as she pleased.

●

"That's crazy! You can't let this go on, you really can't."

This was Suzuki, a classmate of Shiori's. They had been talking about her rather unusual relationship with Nozomi.

Suzuki was Shiori's very first boyfriend. They had been assigned to the same classroom in eleventh grade and started dating in early fall. Shiori found him kind and reliable, and she had the sense she could learn a lot from him.

Though she'd never actually had a chance to interact with Suzuki the previous school year, he had often come up in conversation with her friends—in other words, they had all had their eyes on him. Shiori had never taken an active interest in boys, so her focus on him was unusual.

Back before they landed in the same class, Shiori had called him "Suzuki-kun," adding the *kun* to his family name so she wouldn't sound too brusque, and she went on referring to him that way even now that they knew each other better. Suzuki just used her last name: Hamura.

Shiori's relationship with Suzuki-kun had its good side and its bad side.

All in all, the bad probably outweighed the good. She lost all kinds of important things when they started going out.

She didn't blame him, though. And she didn't regret dating him—far from it. She felt she owed him a lot. True, he did sometimes cast her into despair, but he had also given her a new dream.

That morning, Shiori had come to school with her left arm in a bandage, and Suzuki-kun had kept after her until she confessed what had happened. All through lunch period, she had refused to explain the injury, but on the way home his persistent quizzing finally coaxed the story from her. It only confirmed the negative impression he had of Nozomi.

"That's seriously screwed up," was his response. "And I don't just mean I personally think it's screwed up, it's common sense. I mean, come on. What gives your little sister the right to punish you for singing? And cutting your arm—that's nuts! Like, literally crazy! I don't care if she's your sister, you don't do that. It's wrong. Man, talk about a rotten apple."

It had happened the previous evening, when Shiori was enjoying the afterglow of a long phone call with Suzuki-kun. They had just started dating, and the urge to sing that welled up inside her on a tide of shyness and joy was simply too strong to resist.

By the time she noticed, it was already too late. She was tripping down the stairs, singing. Nozomi, in the living room, gave her yet another tongue-lashing, harsher and more inflexible than ever. She kept repeating that she had no choice but to punish Shiori. And so she went to the kitchen and got a small knife, and cut Shiori's left forearm.

There was quite a lot of blood, but Shiori managed to hide the wound from their parents. Fortunately, their mother was taking a bath, and their father wasn't home yet.

Shiori had no idea how to treat a cut, so for the first few minutes she just kept wiping the blood away with a towel. Eventually it struck her that she probably needed to cover the wound, so she dabbed on some Kip Pyrol and then stuck on a row of Band-Aids.

Still the blood kept oozing out. She put gauze over the wound, then wrapped the gauze in bandages. Finally, things were under control. She hid the bloody towel in her bedroom, so she could wash it when no one was around to see.

Nozomi, who had drawn the knife over Shiori's skin as if it were a magic marker, with no sign of hesitation, seemed unfazed by the sight of so much blood; far from apologizing, she continued to seethe.

After looking on for a while as Shiori struggled to dress the wound, she tossed the knife in the sink and went up to her room. She didn't speak to Shiori for the rest of the evening.

Suzuki-kun was seized with righteous indignation when he heard about all this. He told Shiori he would talk to Nozomi, make her stop. But Shiori defended her sister. Nozomi had been angry, it was a sort of fit, she told him. You shouldn't blame her—it was really my fault for breaking my promise. Besides, Nozomi had said she was sorry at breakfast, so everything was OK now. In reality, Nozomi had never apologized for anything in her life, but in this case a little white lie seemed appropriate.

Shiori was so overjoyed to see Suzuki-kun this concerned—he was angry on her behalf!—that she wouldn't have traded the experience for anything. At the same time, she didn't want him butting into a matter that was really between her and her sister.

However badly Nozomi treated her, Shiori always felt uncomfortable whenever anyone else criticized her sister. She didn't completely understand where that discomfort came from, but she had always felt strongly that she had to protect her younger sister from outside pressures.

Shiori pleaded with Suzuki-kun not to talk to Nozomi, and he finally relented.

"But, so what if you broke your promise?" Suzuki-kun said, clearly disgruntled. "There's nothing wrong with singing. I've never heard anything so stupid."

Suzuki-kun hadn't yet experienced Shiori's singing, so he was unaware of the difficulties she had in this area. Perhaps this made Nozomi's behavior seem more vicious that it otherwise would have. Being the lead singer in a band he had formed may also have inclined him to push back against the notion that Shiori's singing was a crime.

Shiori sensed this as she gazed up at his profile. And she sympathized with his attitude—or with the attitude she imagined was his. In her eyes, she and he were both singers. This was something they shared. She felt she had discovered a vein of purity in the heart of this young man who loved to sing, and this filled her heart with warmth.

I love this about him, she thought.

●

Standing between Nozomi and Suzuki-kun proved to be a tremendous challenge for Shiori, because the two plainly detested one another.

At first, Shiori was too embarrassed to tell Nozomi about her relationship with Suzuki-kun. But you couldn't hide anything from Nozomi—she got wind of their relationship almost immediately after they started dating.

It happened after school on Saturday, October 17. Shiori and Suzuki-kun were hanging out in the CD section of a large supermarket when they ran into Nozomi and her group. Suzuki-kun had some things he wanted to buy, he'd said, and he asked Shiori to come along.

He'd gotten into older rock lately, he said—like, decades old.

"What do you listen to, Hamura?" he asked.

Shiori didn't know what to say. She didn't actually own any CDs; occasionally she listened to albums from her mother's collection of vintage English folk, but that was it. Should she just tell him she liked English folk? No... Somehow that felt wrong, since she hadn't bought those records herself. She also didn't want Suzuki-kun, who was deeply into music and even sang in a band, to know she had never bought a CD. That struck her as a bit unfortunate, seeing as she considered herself a singer, just like him. She was still searching for an answer when a voice broke the silence.

"Shouldn't you just be honest and tell him you don't own any CDs, Shiori?"

There was no need to turn around—Shiori recognized the voice. She couldn't just ignore Nozomi, though, and so, somewhat timidly, she turned to face her.

Nozomi stood with her arms folded, a step closer to Shiori than the other girls. Judging by their uniforms, they were friends from the all-girl school she went to—an institution more competitive than Shiori's and Suzuki-kun's.

Suzuki-kun glanced at Nozomi, then looked back at Shiori. He didn't say anything, but clearly he was wondering who Nozomi was. And so, for the first time ever, Shiori introduced her sister to the boy she was dating.

Nozomi's attitude was brusque, and Suzuki-kun certainly didn't seem pleased, but happily the conversation didn't drag on after the introductions had been made. The pressure of having to deal with Nozomi and Suzuki-kun together had caused Shiori to break out in a cold sweat, but it was done now, at least for the time being. She knew, though, that when she got home Nozomi would question her about everything, prying into every detail.

She was right. The interrogation began after dinner and continued almost until dawn. At first, Shiori tried to deflect Nozomi's demand that she recount the whole step-by-step history of her involvement with Suzuki-kun by protesting that they hadn't even been dating a month, so there was hardly anything to tell. This didn't work. Nozomi simply commanded her once again to talk, and Shiori, easily cowed, couldn't help obeying. Speaking haltingly, blushing, lowering her eyes so she wouldn't have to make eye contact, she told Nozomi everything.

How she had liked him from freshman year, when he was in a different class.

How she had first been drawn to him when she saw him up on stage, singing and playing guitar with his band at the school festival, and how after that she and her girlfriends had started dropping by his classroom between periods and during lunch.

How the two of them had been assigned to the same class in sophomore year, which gave her the chance to chat with him like any other classmate, and then, when the school festival rolled around again, how she had helped his band, and they had started hanging out, sending emails back and forth all day, having long conversations on the phone.

Nozomi responded to all this with an unimpressed sigh.

Then she began sifting through the details. Being in the same class, she suggested, didn't automatically make two people friendly. And you don't just naturally end up going out with a guy because you helped his band. "In other words," she continued, "there are only two possibilities here. Either he came on to you, or you came on to him. Which was it?"

Well... you could say he took the initiative. Shiori did go talk to him sometimes, though, if she had a reason. Early on, she lacked the courage to interact with him unless she needed to, because she was so excitable—she could hardly contain her feelings.

Suzuki-kun must have known Shiori liked him. She had kept turning up with her friends last year when they weren't even in the same class, and now here she was, getting all flustered in front of him... He couldn't have missed it. So, he had treated her the way he would a fan. He chatted with her about his band, his favorite musicians. And when Shiori,

-53-

having somehow missed instructions all the other students had heard, ended up being the only one still sitting bewildered at her desk, he always went over to explain.

Thus, little by little, they had grown closer. He had started it.

"Have you had sex?"

Shiori was used to having her sister pop unexpected questions on her, but this made her start. As it happened, Shiori didn't feel she was ready for sex, and every day she worried that Suzuki-kun might start something. She was stunned that Nozomi had seen so deeply into her heart, since that was what her question implied.

The next moment, Shiori realized she had let herself be shocked too early. She managed to push out a strangled "No," almost biting her tongue in the process, but her answer didn't seem to interest Nozomi. She had something else in mind.

"Oh? You could be lying, though, so I'll have to check." No sooner had Nozomi spoken than she pushed Shiori roughly to the ground and set about stripping off first her sweatpants, then her underwear.

It happened so quickly that at first Shiori didn't even resist; by the time she began kicking, her clothes were already down around her ankles.

"Stop moving, Shiori! What are you doing? Keep still and let me look."

Having extracted Shiori's left foot from her underwear, Nozomi began forcing apart her sister's legs. Naturally, Shiori continued to writhe, struggling to resist, but she could tell from the sheer force Nozomi was bringing to bear on her body that she wasn't playing.

Why is she doing this? Dumb incomprehension flooded Shiori's brain, heightening her anxiety. What was Nozomi looking for? She wasn't a gynecologist. She was so serious that it didn't seem like a prank, but why else would she do it? It made no sense.

"What are you doing, Nozomi?" she demanded.

"Checking your hymen. To see if it's broken."

"Why?"

Nozomi didn't answer, but she did let go. Nozomi was delicately built, and all the rolling around on the floor seemed to have worn her out.

The two sisters lay panting, weighed down by the heavy air.

The crisis had passed, at least for the time being, but still Shiori felt uneasy. She scooted along the floor on her butt, edging away from Nozomi.

"You're tidier than I'd have thought, Shiori. I'm glad to see that."

Shiori could have told her that. She didn't feel ready for sex, but she had been careful to keep nice and clean down there, just in case.

"I didn't see the hymen, but it's OK. I'll give you a pass today—I can see you're not lying. You wouldn't lie to me anyway, I know. But from now on, you've got to keep me informed, OK? That's how sisters are, you know, Shiori darling."

Relived that Nozomi had given up so much more easily than usual, Shiori began pulling up her clothes. As she raised her underwear, though, she noticed that her inner thighs were bright red. She would probably have a bunch of bruises soon.

It would have been nice if Nozomi had relented at this point, but she wasn't going to let Shiori off so lightly. Now that she knew there had been no sex, she turned her attention to kissing.

Shiori and Suzuki-kun had, in fact, kissed. They had first done it last week, and had been doing it with increasing frequency in the days since. Shiori wasn't sure she ought to share this information just yet, however. She had a nasty suspicion that if she admitted to having kissed, Nozomi might start wondering about sex again and attempt another amateur examination. She was still trying to decide how to respond when Nozomi spoke.

"You're not answering. So you've kissed?"

Shiori sensed that the grilling would intensify if she denied this. She nodded.

"Oooh! So you really kissed him, huh?"

Shiori nodded again in response to this blatant attempt to mortify her.

The previous weekend, Suzuki-kun had invited her to the studio where his band rehearsed. It wasn't a real studio, just a prefab shed behind Suzuki-kun's house where they had arranged the drum set, amps, mics, and so on—a sort of improvised practice room. They had covered the walls with posters and stickers from various bands. The floor was lined with cables for the guitars and amps that rose here and there in tall, snake-like coils.

"I've never brought a girl here before," Suzuki-kun told Shiori.

This confession made her very happy. She asked if she could hold one of the guitars, and then a mic—though she managed, with a struggle, to restrain her urge to sing.

After that, as "A Message to Pretty" played over the speakers, their bodies stained red by the rays of the sinking sun, they exchanged a gentle kiss.

Just recalling that precious moment brought tears to Shiori's eyes, emotional troubadour that she was. She took a swig of cola from a can she had brought upstairs with her, hoping the bubbles would distract her, but she swallowed the wrong way and erupted into a fit of coughing.

Nozomi remained dissatisfied even after Shiori recounted this episode.

"How did you kiss him? Show me, Shiori. Kiss me the same way."

"What?" Shiori stiffened.

She had done a lot of kissing over the past few days, but she had never been the one to lean over and press her lips against his. He was always the one to initiate it.

"What's wrong? Come kiss me."

Shiori explained truthfully that she herself had never kissed Suzuki-kun, so she didn't know how to do it. She just let him kiss her.

"You drive me crazy. Look, Shiori, in cases like this, you don't have to be finicky about the details. You could have just come and kissed me. Is it that difficult?"

As she spoke, Nozomi moved her face closer and closer to Shiori's until, at last, their lips touched. Not only did she kiss her, she also folded Shiori in her arms, crushing her own body against hers. As their breasts pressed together, she bent Shiori's head to one side and slipped her tongue into Shiori's mouth.

Shiori let herself be held, and for a few minutes the sisters kissed.

As they drew slowly apart, gazing at each other's flushed faces, Nozomi smiled.

"So? Was it like that?"

Shiori said she wasn't sure. She and Suzuki-kun hadn't kissed that long, or as deeply, but the sensation seemed kind of similar, and so did the feeling it evoked.

In both cases, with Nozomi as with Suzuki-kun, Shiori felt the desire to sing.

There were differences, however. Nozomi's kissing had been more energetic, and Shiori recognized that the emotions bubbling up within her had been different when she was with Suzuki-kun. She couldn't have explained what distinguished them—not in words, at least, although she felt she could have made it clear if she had been allowed to sing.

While Shiori sat lost in her thoughts, Nozomi snatched her cell phone and started reading her emails from Suzuki-kun.

"Hold on, Shiori—you've lent him money?"

Shiori snatched her phone.

"That's private," she said.

Needless to say, Nozomi wasn't one to back down in the face of such a protest.

"It's OK, Shiori. Answer me. Have you given him money?"

Shiori had, indeed, lent Suzuki-kun five thousand yen. It had happened in the CD store, after Nozomi left. In his email, the boy promised to return the money next month.

Suzuki-kun only had a thousand yen in his wallet, Shiori explained. That's why she gave him the money.

"That was dumb," Nozomi said coldly. "You'll never get it back, Shiori."

When Shiori insisted she was wrong, Nozomi heaved a sigh and gave her a look that said, *You don't get it, do you?*

"Listen, Shiori. Don't just sit there with that stunned look on your face—think it through, OK? He asked you to come along to the CD store. Am I right? I mean, that's pretty obvious. You're not likely to invite *him* to go CD shopping."

Shiori was tempted to deny this, but the look in her sister's eye stopped her.

"Any guy who invites a girl to go shopping and then borrows money because he doesn't have it himself is a loser, pure and simple. That's just the worst."

Shiori tried to defend Suzuki-kun, suggesting it was just bad luck that he didn't have the cash on him, but this only egged Nozomi on.

"I don't understand, I really don't. How can you have such faith in a guy like him, who looks every bit the loser he is? I'm telling you, Shiori, people will take advantage of you forever if you keep thinking that way. *Please* tell me you didn't lend him any money before you started dating. You didn't do *that*, did you?"

She had. Just a few times, and it was never all that much, but... Shiori thought it might make things worse to mention that now. She started to shake her head, but already it was too late. Nozomi could spot the slightest hesitation.

"OK, so you did. Everything's clear now. You may believe you're his girlfriend, Shiori, but that's not how he sees it. As far as he's concerned, you're just a pot of money. I don't know if he's aware of it or not, but basically the guy is a pimp. You let things go on like this, Shiori, and you'll just be his piggybank. Maybe you don't think it's a big deal, five thousand yen for a couple CDs, but wait and see. Next month he'll have you footing the bill for a five-hundred-thousand-yen guitar. Listen, Shiori, this isn't advice I'm giving you here, it's a prediction. That's exactly what's going to happen, I'm telling you. You've got to end this relationship—send this jerk packing. It's not like you've got much of a relationship to begin with, so ending it won't be that hard."

Why did Nozomi always take such extreme and arbitrary positions? How could she treat a guy she had met for the first time today, and with whom she had hardly spoken, in such a dismissive, one-sided way? She was always like this, of course, but this time Shiori found it harder than usual to accept her brash, unreasonable attitude. And so, pulling herself together, she managed to offer a rebuttal. It wasn't right to say such mean things about Suzuki-kun, she said, when Nozomi didn't even know him.

"I could say exactly the same the same to you, Shiori. How much do you know about him? I don't mean his blood type or his zodiac sign, favorite foods, hobbies—all the crap people put in their profiles. I'm asking how deeply you've peered into the wicked heart of this conniving bastard. Frankly, I don't think you understand him at all. It's true I've only met him once, but I guarantee I've summed him up better than you have. You may get together with him at school every day, but no girl as blissfully ignorant as you could possibly see what he's up to. Besides, you're in love with him, right? Your little eyes get all clouded over with romance and, bam, that's it—even a dumb loser like him can walk all over you."

Shiori insisted that Nozomi had it all wrong, that they trusted each other because they shared a genuine emotional connection, but Nozomi wasn't having any of it.

"You're a dreamer, Shiori, and that's just another of your cute little dreams. Sure, he tells you he likes you, he's crazy about you, whatever, and you fall for it, and he showers you with kisses until you start thinking you've got this bond, that's what you're telling yourself—but the truth is, these things have an outside and an inside. You never try to look beyond the outside—in fact you don't even believe there *is* an inside—so the most transparent charlatan has no problem gaining your trust. Even if you get burned, you still don't face up to reality, you just go on listening to your heart. The truth is, you never actually communicate with anyone, you're just talking at them in your own fantasy world. You don't see others as being separate from you, you've decided everyone feels the same things you do, and with the same intensity, so, when you find yourself a boyfriend, you don't bother to try and imagine what he might be after, and have no doubt he'll always be there by your side, sharing everything. That, in a nutshell, is the kind of person you are, Shiori. You're the perfect representative of that type. And that's what makes it so easy for a worthless poser like him to exploit you. Poor girl."

Listening to this speech, Shiori couldn't help feeling that Nozomi herself deserved to be pitied. She was so wrapped up in her cynicism that she based every interaction on the presumption of evil intentions. Her view of the world was all wrong.

Looking at things this way, assuming the fundamental depravity of human nature, would only lead her into increasing isolation, and having to remain constantly on guard against the iniquity she saw all around her would keep her from ever finding peace.

Shiori couldn't understand how her sister's view of the world had come to be so jaded. How could she and Nozomi, living under the same roof, have come to look at humankind so differently? Had Nozomi endured some terrible experience, the damage from which she kept concealed deep within her? If so, surely it was Shiori's responsibility to be there for her in her need. And so, trying her hardest to be casual, she asked Nozomi very gently if anything had happened at school to hurt her.

Nozomi responded with a smile as tender as the Virgin Mary's.

"That's a very thoughtful response for you, Shiori. I see you've understood, at least a little, how important it is to adopt that kind of a questioning attitude. You deserve praise for that, I'll be the first to acknowledge it—though I'm afraid that still won't get you a passing grade. Didn't I just say that not everyone is like you? People's philosophies don't always stem from their life experiences. You can experience all kinds of things, and analyze to death everything that happens to you, but if you're not the sort of person who is capable of being transformed by such things, they won't change you. Dad likes to say that only death cures a fool. In the end, it all depends on how you use your brain. Maybe you can't do much in that area because that's not how you're made, but even so I'd like you to remember just one thing. Always consider people's inner motives—that's the core of social life. If you can manage that, you'll have all the communication skills you need. Conversation gets more and more interesting to the extent that you can draw on various techniques to anticipate what people are going to say. You don't need life experience or books to tell you that—we've been passing this knowledge down implicitly from ancient times. It's common sense in every field from politics to business. If you get angry over having been tricked, people will assume you're either dumb or naive. The world is full of people who've fallen prey to charlatans, and superficially, at least, we pretend we sympathize, but in our heart of hearts we think they're fools. That's just how it is. So you have to learn to fit your attitude to the context—really, that's the most basic thing. Any minimally competent person who realizes she's been tricked will set about mastering the same technique herself and then go try it out on someone else. We humans just keep repeating that process, everyone imitating everyone else… That's how we've built up whole societies and cultures and economies. In that sense, the game this guy is playing with you is entirely legitimate. It's just that his approach is so pathetic and cheap, and it pisses me off to see you being taken in by such a piece of trash. So here's the deal. Though I'd like to see you break up with him immediately—tomorrow, if possible—I can't bear to have you do that until you've set a trap for him. What do you think, Shiori? Naturally, I'm willing to help. How about it? What should we do?"

Shiori didn't know what to say. All she could do was keep shaking her head, again and again, as tears streamed down her cheeks. She didn't agree with anything Nozomi had said. That whole long, brutal lecture had accomplished nothing other than to make her feel so miserable it seemed her chest might crack.

Nozomi regarded her sobbing sister with narrowed eyes. By now Shiori had actually begun to quake, as if from fear. Evidently concluding that this was a moment to comfort her sister, Nozomi stroked Shiori's head, then all of a sudden leaned over and hugged her.

"Go on, cry it all out. I know, I know. You can always cry in front of me, as much as you like. Cry like a baby, bawl your eyes out—it's OK. There's no one here but you and me."

The younger sister gave the elder sister a kiss. Then, raising her lips, Nozomi licked away what remained of the tears on Shiori's cheeks, her tongue darting in and out of her mouth like a cat's. She sat back and watched, as if hoping for a fresh crop of tears.

●

It was almost inevitable that Suzuki-kun would dislike Nozomi. Shiori hadn't reproduced the conversation with her in detail for him, but he had reasons of his own to regard her as an enemy. The Monday after Nozomi learned Shiori and Suzuki-kun were dating, she started trying to get in their way.

Since Nozomi attended a different high school, she couldn't keep them apart completely. After school let out, though, she did everything she could. She would call Shiori on her cell phone and demand to know where she was, then come and force herself on the couple, monopolizing her older sister and making snide, sarcastic comments at Suzuki-kun's expense. Sometimes she brought her classmates along so they could all ridicule him together, making sure he was within earshot.

After three days of this, Suzuki-kun took Shiori by the hand after class and led her off somewhere they wouldn't be found. He even made her turn off her phone.

Shiori returned home slightly past six that evening. She opened the front door with some trepidation, but Nozomi was upstairs in her bedroom, talking with friends, so she managed to get inside without incident.

When Nozomi's friends left, she watched TV in the living room, and then she and Shiori took their places at the kitchen table and had cabbage rolls for dinner. Even then, nothing much happened—perhaps because their mother was there, too.

Except that Nozomi had already exacted a small revenge.

Just as Shiori was finishing up, her phone started ringing on the sofa. After confirming that it was, in fact, Suzuki-kun, she dashed excitedly up the stairs, her heart thumping in her chest. Nothing in his tone suggested that his feelings matched hers, however: he was so cold that he sounded like an altogether different person from the one she had left earlier. Shiori ended up spending the next two hours in her room, placating him.

Needless to say, it was Nozomi who'd put him in that foul mood. She had waited until Shiori went into the kitchen to help with dinner, then sent him an abusive email from Shiori's phone which she'd signed with Shiori's name. She included a made-up explanation for why Shiori was writing an email like this now, making it hard for Suzuki-kun to tell what was true and how he ought to respond. Nozomi, the email said, had been trying to keep Shiori and Suzuki-kun apart for a reason: the truth was that Shiori had no desire to be involved with him, but since he wasn't getting the message, Shiori had asked her sister to do something, anything, to make him give up on her. Evidently that plan hadn't worked, either, so she had made up her mind to write to him herself...

After much earnest explanation, Shiori succeeded in persuading Suzuki-kun that it was all a misunderstanding. Still, she couldn't stop him from calling Nozomi "that damned girl" and cursing her out in no uncertain terms as, without any warning, he began pouring out all the resentments that had piled up inside him over the past few days.

It took all Shiori had not to burst into tears as she replied, but she tried her best to soothe him, and when he finally calmed down and said something nice, telling her not to worry, he wouldn't stop liking her over something like this, she felt so relieved to hear the strength of their bond in his words that she finally did cry.

All this took an hour. The second hour was the opposite of the first, dedicated to pleasant conversation and saccharine comments of the sort couples are wont to make. Shiori was so reassured and happy to be free of the sourness that had hung in the air ten minutes earlier that she felt as if she were dreaming. Suzuki-kun, too, got caught up in the moment and began saying all sorts of things meant to appeal to her romantic nature.

In the end, however, this brought on another catastrophe. Shiori was so elated when she hung up that she immediately burst into song. And that led Nozomi to cut her arm.

Suzuki-kun's animosity toward Nozomi reached fever pitch when he learned what was behind Shiori's injury. Though he agreed not to confront Nozomi directly, he complained forcibly to Shiori on the way home from school. Nozomi's actions, he said, were absolutely incomprehensible. Swept up in his anger, he went so far as to begin analyzing her psychology, delving into her twisted personality in a tone so passionate she might have been a riddle he'd grown obsessed with solving.

Maybe, he suggested, she was trying to end their relationship because she couldn't get a boyfriend herself? Shiori found this rather simplistic theory unpersuasive. Judging from his expression as he glanced at Shiori, who was gazing at him with a quizzical look on her face, he seemed to sense that he had missed the mark.

It was true Nozomi didn't have a boyfriend, but she had so many guys asking her out that she would have needed a broom to get rid of them all. She wasn't easy to get along with, and you couldn't beat her in an argument, but there was no denying she was extremely cute—she came across as a gorgeous, incredibly smart, lively girl. Ever since she was young, she had stood out, in ways both good and bad; people naturally gravitated toward her, though she didn't have a single really intimate friend. She loved to win, but she always seemed slightly detached; there was something childish in her looks, but she behaved like an adult.

Being her older sister, Shiori regarded Nozomi at times with annoyance and at others with pride. Nozomi was more beautiful than anyone in her eyes. Above all, Shiori loved the little things she did with her body, seemingly without even realizing it. Nozomi hated physicality, but she carried herself so gracefully and elegantly that it became a means of expression... or so it seemed to Shiori. She had always envied Nozomi for this.

Thinking about Nozomi this way made Shiori want to burst out singing. But Suzuki-kun was right next to her, and they were in public, surrounded by other people. Singing was out of the question. She began to fidget instead.

Soon Suzuki-kun turned to her with a slightly sheepish expression on his face. His mood had improved now that he had said what he thought of Nozomi, and his tone was gentle.

"Want to come back to my house? There's no school tomorrow."

Their school had Saturday classes only every other week, and this wasn't one of those weeks. He had said the same thing a fortnight ago, when he invited her to his studio.

"Sure." Shiori gave a little nod. Maybe if she was lucky, he would take her to the rehearsal space again, and he might let her sing a little, even if it were just a whisper.

Suzuki-kun led Shiori straight to the studio, just like last time. The prospect that she might get to sing made it hard for her to keep still; Suzuki-kun, too, seemed oddly nervous.

He put on a random CD and sat on a stool, cradling his electric guitar, which he hadn't plugged in.

"Yeah, this is the kind of music I want to play," he said, tilting his head toward the speaker and strumming the strings.

He didn't sound like he meant it. He talked about this and that, running through the titles of the songs he'd be practicing with the band over the weekend, but his mind seemed to be elsewhere.

"You're welcome to sit down," he told her.

The thought of singing made Shiori so jittery she couldn't contain herself, though, and she kept wandering here and there around the small room. Hoping he might realize what she was so eager to do, she planted herself in front of the mic. She blushed as she imagined him asking her to sing.

Outside, the sun had nearly set. According to the calendar, the first day of winter was only two weeks off, but it didn't feel particularly cool in the prefab shed. Evidently no one else was home, because the main house was silent, and there were none of the gusts of wind that often blew at this time of year. The only sound was the syrupy English-language rock playing over the speakers.

It struck Shiori that she hadn't met anyone from Suzuki-kun's family last time she was here, either. She was just about to ask where everyone was when he strode over and covered her lips with his.

They had been kissing a lot these days, but he had never come on to her this suddenly. It felt different, too—more intense. Even after their lips parted, he stayed as he was, pressed up against her. Then, ever so slowly, he began touching her, exploring her body with his hands. Shiori sensed that if they kept heading in this direction, they would almost certainly end up having sex.

Suzuki-kun kept roving passionately over her body, first here, then there, saying nothing. His agitated breathing came to sound like a sort of music, heightening the temptation to give voice to her troubadour nature. Perhaps as a result, she could no longer call up the vision she had replayed so often in her mind as she strove to prepare herself for this moment. After all the time she had spent thinking through precisely how she would accept his advances, she had forgotten her plan. Unsure how to proceed, she stood stock still with her arms bent, like a runner at the starting line.

Suzuki-kun, clearly too aroused to notice her bewilderment, concentrated on her lower body. Standing there like that, he seemed a bit like a pervert on a train. Gradually the sound of his increasingly lusty breathing was elevated in Shiori's mind, transformed into pure song. Neither of them noticed when the CD ended; the only sounds to be heard in the studio were their breathing and the friction of their clothes rubbing together.

And so it came to pass that Shiori sang for Suzuki-kun.

She did not, however, sing for very long.

Suzuki-kun, who was obviously taken aback, seemed not to have grasped that she was singing. Believing, perhaps, that she had simply yelped, he stopped what he had been doing.

"Sorry," he said gently. "That hurt?"

Shiori shook her head. It hadn't hurt.

It seemed odd to be standing, so Suzuki-kun brought over a stool and suggested that Shiori sit down. She obeyed. The moment she settled onto the seat, Suzuki-kun's expression relaxed. Evidently he read this as a sign she was willing to proceed.

Suzuki-kun knelt down before Shiori and parted her legs. He took the hem of her skirt in his hands and began slowly lifting it up. Just as he was about to expose her upper thighs, he glanced up to gauge her reaction, a childlike look on his face. Shiori was too embarrassed to meet his gaze.

When he had hoisted her skirt all the way up to her waist, revealing not only her thighs but also her blue-striped underwear, he touched her with his cold palms, making her shudder. Then she felt his warm breath on the inside of her thighs—first the right, then the left—and once again she started. He froze for a few seconds. She imagined him ogling her body, and felt her neck grow warm.

"What's this?" Suzuki-kun asked, lifting his face.

Looking down, she saw that he was inspecting two enormous bruises on her legs. A sigh escaped her lips as she remembered the scene the previous weekend; then she fell silent. The image of Nozomi peeling off her underwear and forcing her legs apart so she could confirm that she was still a virgin came back to her so clearly that she got mixed up and inhaled when she should have exhaled.

Just like that, like a stereo being flicked off, the intimate mood that hung in the air was wrecked; the sensual warmth that had enveloped Shiori's body faded. Suzuki-kun's eyes, staring up at her, betrayed his confusion.

Shiori's bruises were always slow to heal, and, even though these were a week old, they were still clearly visible. Obviously Shiori couldn't tell Suzuki-kun the truth about how she had gotten them, since she didn't want to prejudice him further against Nozomi, so she told him she had fallen off her bike.

He seemed unconvinced by their brief discussion of the subject, but he didn't probe. He drew his own conclusions, then muttered an awkward "Sorry" before lowering her skirt and clambering to his feet. He stuck a cigarette in his mouth and started the CD player.

Shiori had ruined the atmosphere. She felt so bad she wanted to cry. She knew, though, that they would both feel much worse if she did. Her mind raced to come up with something she could say, but she just felt more and more like a failure, and in the end she had no choice but to keep quiet.

Eventually, Suzuki-kun broke the silence.

"I thought I'd been too rough, you know? Like maybe I bumped you somehow."

Shiori shook her head again and told him it really hadn't hurt.

"Anyway, there's no point doing stuff here, with all this crap around. I was getting ahead of myself. I'm still kind of green, I guess."

He apologized once more and smiled. Shiori answered with a smile of her own. He really was a nice guy, she thought, somewhat relieved.

"I'm sorry my singing made you think I was hurt," she said.

"Your singing? Like, a song?"

Shiori nodded.

"I didn't realize. So that was you singing, huh?"

Suzuki-kun's expression suddenly turned grave, and he fell silent. Shiori waited anxiously to hear what he would say next.

"Now that you mention it, I've never heard you sing. Not even once. What's up with that? Don't you think you should sing for me sometime? You like singing, right?"

Shiori felt as if someone had dropped a weight on her stomach, but in a way that was somehow pleasant.

"Me?" she said simply.

"Yeah. You like to sing, right? C'mon, then. Sing for me."

Shiori fluttered her hands like she did when she said good-bye to her girlfriends, making a nominal display of embarrassment. Her body brimmed with a marvelous warmth.

"Don't be shy! It's fine, I want to hear you. Your sister might cut you again if you sing at home—better get it out here. We've got a mic and everything. C'mon, let's hear it."

At last, the moment had arrived. Shiori had been praying for this, and now an unexpected turn of events had made it happen exactly the way she had wanted. All of a sudden, she was living her dream. She had never asked if she could sing for him, only imagined it, and yet it had all played out exactly as she hoped. Clearly some force beyond human understanding had intervened on her behalf.

Such were the thoughts streaking like sparks through Shiori's brain. She felt as if heaven had granted her an unexpected bounty, and she was touched, overwhelmed with gratitude. She yearned to offer up a heartfelt prayer of thanks to the God of Troubadours and decided to fashion her gratitude into a song.

So eager was she to begin singing her thanks that she couldn't even wait for Suzuki-kun to adjust the volume on the mic. She just belted it out. Numb with joy, she let loose a sort of hymn in her own particular style, as though she had been transformed into a gospel singer, mixing up bits of real songs with music of her own creation, allowing her true troubadour colors to shine. She clasped her hands in front of her, closed her eyes and threw open her mouth, adopting the attitude of a pious singer. She planned to keep singing until the poetry welling within her had subsided.

Ultimately, Suzuki-kun stopped her before she reached that point. She had sung with more abandon than she had in ages, though—indeed, this could well have been the first time in her life that she had dived so deeply into her music and expressed her feelings with such honesty, either alone or in the presence of others.

Born troubadour that she was, Shiori could not have anticipated that this first experience would also be her last.

All at once, she felt herself being shaken. She stopped singing. Suzuki-kun had grabbed her by the shoulders and was whipping her forward and back, his expression frighteningly stiff and tinged with desperation.

Shiori was startled, but she was so overjoyed that she'd had a chance to sing at the top of her lungs for the first time in her life that Suzuki-kun's rude behavior didn't offend her at all. She felt so wonderful, in fact, that she even asked, as she struggled to catch her breath, what he thought.

Tell me honestly, she said. Suzuki-kun folded his arms and thought. Then, in a tone that suggested he would rather not have to comment, his face so flushed that he looked as if he might suffocate, he said:

"You're singing is… well… original, I'd say."

"How so?" Shiori asked eagerly, pleased with the compliment. "In what way?"

Irritation flickered across Suzuki-kun's face; then, frowning, he scratched the back of his head. Finally, emerging from some internal struggle, he replied:

"Listen, I'm going to be honest. You're not a good singer, Hamura. I'd say you're kind of on the bad side, actually. You're tone deaf. Like, really bad tone deafness. Hey, look, I'm in a band myself, right, and I sing, so I don't want to fool around with stuff like this, to tell you you're great. I'm not going to lie. You asked me to be honest, and I feel like if I tried to be nice here, I'd just make things worse. You can see that, right? Anyway, that's the truth. You're not a good singer. At the same time, you've got something interesting—I really believe that. It's just not singing, you know? It's something else."

It was all Shiori could do to hold back her tears. She had to concentrate very hard, and it took a lot out of her. In all her seventeen years on this planet, she had never once been as deeply hurt as she was then. And yet she still managed to pinch her face into a smile, so she wouldn't make Suzuki-kun worry. She kept blinking, again and again, as she tried not to seem like she was crying. Two or three tears ran down her cheek, but she lowered her face quickly enough that Suzuki-kun didn't even notice.

"Did I upset you? If so, I'm sorry. I'm doing a lot of apologizing today, huh?"

"You haven't upset me at all," Shiori said, forcing herself to stay strong. "This has been good for me, actually—you told me the truth. I'm tone deaf."

These words shredded her soul, but she endured. Her vision grew blurry; her body went so limp she almost crumpled to the floor—but still she endured.

●

Shiori cried all the way home.

There wasn't much traffic on the rural road, but she passed a few people along the way. Whenever people drew near, they would stop and listen. Some showed their concern by asking gently if she was OK, but even they seemed, on some level, to have fallen under the spell of her strangely beautiful sobs. Shiori didn't accept their help; she simply told them she was fine and trudged on, pushing her bicycle beside her.

Shiori had been so devastated when Suzuki-kun told her she was tone deaf that she didn't know how she would ever recover. Now more than ever, she needed to be comforted by the parakeets. But alas, it was not to be—by the time she got to the supermarket, the clerks were already closing up. Shiori crouched beside her bicycle outside the darkened building, in a vast parking lot that was empty aside from a few cars, and hung her head and cried and cried until she felt she had cried enough.

The only bright point in all this was that Nozomi stayed out late again that night with her school friends, so Shiori was able to spend some time alone, thinking about herself and who she was, without her sister making sport of her misery.

Shiori and Suzuki-kun had exchanged a few emails and talked on the phone since she left his house. She always pretended she was all right. He might as well have handed her a death sentence, but it wasn't his fault. He had told the truth, that was all—an incredibly painful truth, yes, but still. After all, she was the one who had asked his opinion.

She detested herself. No one but Suzuki-kun had ever told her she was tone deaf—no one, that is, but Nozomi, who had once referred to her singing as "empty noise." Maybe Suzuki-kun was tone deaf, not her? It was possible, though it was hard to see how this could be the case, since he sang in a band. And when she remembered how people had responded to her singing in the past, she had to admit he was probably right. People had never said to her face that she was tone deaf, but in retrospect certain comments they had made and things they had done showed that this was what they had been thinking. *All along, people were trying to tell me I can't sing,* she realized, *but I'm so dumb I never got the message.* Not only had she persuaded herself she was destined to live with music, but she had actually ignored all these hints people kept dropping, even brushing off her sister's explicit warnings. Objectively, she could see that this was what she had done.

Ever since she was little, everyone, without exception, had reacted badly to her singing. The question was: Why, faced with all this rejection, had she failed to realize she was utterly and completely tone deaf?

Shiori kept beating herself up.

She was an oblivious, dull, egotistical, stupid girl with absolutely no ability to hold a tune, who had nonetheless let herself get swept up in this ludicrous fantasy of being a troubadour. As a result, all her life she had been harming the people around her. Obviously she could no longer consider herself a troubadour, now that she knew she couldn't sing. Maybe it would be best if she gave up on everything else, too.

Shiori made up her mind to die. She left home on Sunday afternoon, thinking maybe she would ride her bicycle down a dangerously busy street, or find a tall building to jump from. First, though, she realized she needed to go visit the parakeets.

The supermarket was busier that Sunday evening than it had been whenever she'd stopped by on the way home from school, but to Shiori, wrapped up as she was in thoughts of dying, the customers looked like figures on a painted backdrop at a play. It wouldn't have been surprising if she had run into one or two friends or acquaintances, but she wasn't even collected enough to plan a response in case a classmate noticed her and said hello.

Though Shiori was despondent and prepared to die, she wasn't exactly opposed to living. Until now, suicide had been as far from her thoughts as it could possibly have been, and she was terrified of dying. Yet here she was, being dragged almost out of the blue, unwillingly, down the path to self-annihilation. She didn't *want* to die; it was as though her body itself was determined to destroy her consciousness. She was horribly afraid, but the despair of losing her troubadour identity had left such a void in her that she could no longer really control herself or think rationally.

That was why she had come here, to stand before these cages: she was hoping fervently that the parakeets might have the power to save her. She had faith in them—faith that they could raise her from the swamp of her suicidal impulses.

It had been a whole week since she last visited the birds. Ever since she and Suzuki-kun started dating, she had been hanging out with him after school, and with each passing day her attachment to the pet shop had weakened. She was shocked to see how many of the cages were gone. While she had been out enjoying life with her new boyfriend, the parakeets were steadily being sold off. One by one, they had been losing their friends. This realization made Shiori hate herself even more.

Sure, it was only to be expected. These birds were here to be sold as pets. But it still hurt that so many, more than half, had disappeared during the precise period when she and Suzuki-kun had become intimate.

"I'm so sorry," Shiori murmured tearfully to the few remaining birds, since there was nothing else she could do. She was ashamed of her own selfishness, seeking out these fragile creatures, free only within the confines of their cages, only when she needed their help.

I'm so sorry. She had spoken these same words to them countless times before. The birds always responded with a delightful explosion of screeching. Perhaps they had learned to recognize the sounds.

Shiori listened to the shrill *gyaa gyaa* of the parakeets' familiar cry, her heart swelling with so much love that it hurt.

"Thank you," she murmured again, as tearfully as before.

The birds chirped back, happy to continue the conversation. Shiori was so touched she almost burst into song, but she stopped herself at the last moment.

No, that's not quite accurate. She hadn't intentionally arrested her singing; she had found, as she was about to release the first note, that she simply couldn't produce a sound. She tensed her stomach, but nothing came. Something inside her hit the brakes.

It doesn't matter. I'm not going to sing anyway.

Now that she had arrived at this point, the sense of loss was so tremendous it stopped up her tear ducts, and rather than feel empty she simply gave up. So she couldn't sing; what did that matter? She could still talk. She could live her day-to-day life just as well.

She stayed at the pet shop until closing time.

As she listened to the birds, her death wish began to fade, its place being taken little by little by the will to go on living. No doubt the clerks were irked by her presence, but they never asked her to leave—she was a good customer, after all, and she was careful never to interfere with the other customers. They just looked the other way.

By the time she left the store and headed home, she was feeling profoundly grateful, both to the parakeets and to Suzuki-kun. The birds had cheered her up, giving her new hope after the dejection she had felt when she left the house; Suzuki-kun had given her the hint that triggered this transformation within her.

She was still down, of course, but she hadn't forgotten what Suzuki-kun said after he told her she was tone deaf. *You've got something interesting—I really believe that. It's just not singing, you know? It's something else.*

She had to find that "something else." That was her true destiny.

Three days later, she had a new dream—she would be a lyricist. She was still destined to live with music. She was a troubadour who couldn't sing.

●

Nozomi's interference wasn't entirely to blame for Shiori's decision to stop seeing Suzuki-kun. Several other factors had opened a gap between them.

They finally agreed to part ways once and for all on Christmas Eve, but their relationship had already started to sour a month before that. Various signs indicated that things were not going well. Shiori's recognition that she was tone deaf had really set the process in motion; but things had been happening at school, too: an odd rumor started making the rounds, and her friends began acting weirdly stand-offish with her, sometimes even genuinely cold, leading Shiori to start withdrawing from all the people around her, just as she had in middle school.

Each of these events caused Shiori some degree of suffering, but the most shocking and painful was an unsettling incident that took place one day when she went to the pet shop with Suzuki-kun.

For some time after Suzuki-kun told her she was tone deaf, Shiori had forced herself to act almost overly chipper in his presence. Not content merely to put on a happy face, she went out of her way to be gregarious and open, so that he might understand her. Ever since that evening at his house, though, she had occasionally sensed a new sharpness in his interactions with her, though it was hard to put a finger on precisely what it was. She tried to tell herself she was over-thinking things, being paranoid, but she couldn't help it: every little thing he did seemed pregnant with significance, and she just couldn't shake her pessimism.

Could it be, she thought, *that without even meaning to, I'm acting as if he hurt my feelings? So he feels like he has to be extra considerate, to keep his thoughts to himself?*

She was constantly in the grip of these abject musings, and, as a result, she became all the more theatrical in his presence.

As time passed, Shiori also began accommodating herself more and more to Suzuki-kun's wishes. She no longer found it so easy to drop by the pet shop after school to enjoy a few minutes with her parakeets, and of course she had forbidden herself to sing, so her emotions grew increasingly unstable.

One Friday after school, she managed to persuade Suzuki-kun to come to the pet shop after they went together to look at CDs. After agreeing to lend him the five thousand yen he always asked for, she suggested fearfully that, in exchange, once he had bought the CDs, perhaps he might be willing to go down to the pet shop on the first floor.

She knew Suzuki-kun was too generous to refuse, but, even so, she waited with her head lowered for his reply, not wanting to see his expression cloud over for even an instant. She was happy when he replied with a simple "Sure."

Having been away from the parakeets for five full days, Shiori felt a mixture of joy and guilt as they stepped into the elevator to descend to the first floor. Thrilled at the prospect of finally being able to share the parakeets' sweet chirping with Suzuki-kun, her mind raced as she searched for a good way to introduce the cute, colorful birds.

As they left the elevator, she summoned the courage to take his hand and lead him on, walking so fast she was almost running. Her palm was clammy with sweat.

She paused for a moment at the entrance to the pet shop, which took up one side of the vast store. Then, by way of introducing the topic, she told Suzuki-kun that there were some really adorable parakeets in the store.

"Ah. Oh?" Suzuki-kun nodded. He made no effort to continue the conversation, though, or meet Shiori's eye. Instead, he scanned their surroundings, as if trying to feign an interest he didn't feel. You could almost hear him muttering to himself, "What a pain in the ass."

Shiori didn't let any of this worry her; she forced herself to take him by the hand again, dragging him deeper into the store.

Maybe she should have turned back. A few times in her life, Shiori had seen things that beggared belief; the scene that met her eyes now added one to the total. The birds were gone. The cages where her tiny friends had lived were empty—in fact, only a few of the cages were left, and they had been marked for sale. It wasn't just the parakeets, either. There wasn't a single bird anywhere.

Shiori searched the entire store, wandering in circles with tears in her eyes like a baby lost in a subterranean tunnel, but they were nowhere to be found. There was no birdsong, either. None of that wonderful chirping that had soothed her soul.

A male clerk walked over, recognizing her as a regular and sensing from her pallor and the look of bewilderment on her face that something was amiss.

"Is something wrong?" he asked.

"Did someone buy all the parakeets?" she said, her voice trembling.

"No," he replied without missing a beat, his tone firm and stern. "No one bought them." He looked directly at Shiori. "They all died. The parakeets, the sparrows, the canaries... over the past few days, all our birds died. We're still trying to figure out why."

It occurred to Shiori that the clerk was speaking like a newscaster. For some reason he seemed to be glaring at her, an accusatory glint in his eyes. She found this very unnerving.

What kind of person had bought the parakeets? She imagined a rich bird lover, hoping it was someone like that. Once again, she suppressed her fear and asked the clerk if it had been someone wealthy. But however she rephrased the question, the reality of what had happened remained the same, and so did his answer.

"I told you, they died. Every last one. We may have to close the store. I'm sure we will if it turns out it was some sort of epidemic. That's a possibility—it did get every one of them. If it wasn't disease, there's a chance some awful person did it. Someone could have poisoned their feed. Obviously, we'll want to track the person down if that's the case. Either way, we're facing really substantial losses."

Shiori heard a ringing in her ears, and suddenly her field of vision narrowed. Then, as if both her legs and her hips had given out beneath her, she collapsed.

Suzuki-kun had been peering blankly into a tank filled with tropical fish known as "black ghosts" when he saw what had happened and rushed over. He knelt down beside Shiori, and he and the clerk carefully lifted her to a sitting position.

They're all dead, she thought. And with that, the dam holding back her emotions crumbled, and she burst into tears. She felt as if her wailing would fill the supermarket, but in fact the sound was no louder than a whisper.

The two men cradled her like an invalid, rubbing her back. From time to time, as she sat with her tear-streaked face buried in her hands, she emitted a raspy moan.

Everything was black, even in the cracks between her fingers.

The men's voices were like echoes from a distant mountain. The blood had drained from her face, she was freezing cold, and she felt as isolated and alone as a climber who had lost her way on a snow-covered peak.

The moment Suzuki-kun and the clerk began debating whether or not to call an ambulance, however, she came to. She scrambled to her feet, afraid things were about to get out of hand, assuring them it was just an anemic spell and she would be fine if she could just rest for a bit in the supermarket's medical office. When she had lain down for about an hour, Suzuki-kun walked her partway home. She went the rest of the way herself.

She stayed home for four days, including the weekend. She doubted she would have felt any better even if she had skipped another whole week of school, but she figured she ought to go back. She had caused Suzuki-kun enough trouble and anxiety already.

During her four-day break, Shiori hadn't simply stayed holed up in her room, wallowing in her depression. In her own way, she understood that there was no point giving herself up to self-loathing and insecurity. Above all, she felt acutely that the deaths of those poor little birds were on her.

Maybe it was her singing. Maybe that was what killed them.

Maybe I'm the murderer who destroyed those birds.

All day Saturday, she was tortured by this thought. Gripped by the irrational notion that she might be to blame for the misfortune that had befallen them, she trembled in the face of her sin. The precise cause of death didn't matter; ultimately, it was her fault. Forcing them to listen to her tone-deaf singing like that had been a terrible thing to do.

On Sunday, she entered a new stage. An accusatory voice boomed in her mind: *For the rest of your life, you must live with this sin.*

Having accepted this reality, she spent the next two days considering how to make amends.

Nozomi was right—you're a criminal. So for the time being, at least, it's only right that you accept her punishments.

In the wake of this new revelation, Shiori confessed to Nozomi what had happened and asked her sister to chastise her.

"I admire your forthrightness, Shiori," Nozomi replied, and promptly agreed to give Shiori what she desired.

"Let me see... I guess since you told me on your own, I can let you off lightly this time. I won't be so strict."

Nozomi ordered Shiori to erase everything that had to do with Suzuki-kun from her phone. She would also have to block his number so she wouldn't get his calls or emails.

"That just prevents you from communicating by phone, so it's really not much of a punishment. It's like a suspended sentence, since you'll see him at school anyway. You should be grateful that you have such a generous sister. But since I'm being so nice, I don't want you secretly unblocking his number or recovering the data or anything, OK? If I catch you doing stuff like that, you can forget the suspended sentence. I'll *really* punish you then."

Shiori obeyed her sister. Not because she was afraid of the consequences, but because she wanted to. She was the one who had asked Nozomi to punish her.

Only after she made up her mind to spend the rest of her life atoning for her sins, which she felt was her duty, did Shiori decide she could return to school. That same accusing voice in her head told her she couldn't atone for anything while staying holed up at home, and that she really ought to thank Suzuki-kun for all he had done, and apologize.

Further trials awaited her at school, however.

During her two days at home, Monday and Tuesday, a rumor that she had been raped had made the rounds at school. She didn't hear about it until Thursday, but even before then she noticed that some of the girls in her grade seemed oddly stand-offish.

Her friend Hinako, who had been in her class last year and was part of the group that used to go to Suzuki-kun's classroom, told her what people were saying. The rumor included the fact that Shiori had two large bruises on her thighs.

Shiori couldn't help smiling when it dawned on her that this was probably how the story started—evidently someone had seen the bruises. She kept grinning as she assured Hinako there was no need to worry, explaining in a general way that she had gotten the bruises horsing around with her sister.

There was no way to dispel the rumor, though, now that it had spread. It was here to stay.

These days, Shiori thought she could detect a slight edge in Suzuki-kun's interactions with her, though he wasn't avoiding her, and the rumor didn't actually appear to have registered with him at all. So they carried on just the same as before, chatting between classes, enjoying each other's company during lunch and after school, chilling with his band at a café. Suzuki-kun still borrowed money to buy CDs and supplies for his guitar, too.

The one issue Suzuki-kun complained about was her inability to communicate by phone. Shiori didn't tell him this was a punishment; she just said her phone had broken and left him to make the best of it.

The rumor made more of an impact on the other students, however. Day by day, they withdrew from Shiori, with those in her grade becoming particularly cold; before long, she found that Suzuki-kun and Hinako were the only ones she could talk with freely. She tried to tell herself it didn't matter, that as long as she had the two of them she was OK, but by the end of November even these last two relationships were fraying.

Hinako set things in motion by telling Shiori she thought Suzuki-kun himself had started the rumor about the rape. It made sense, of course. He had gotten a good look at the bruises on her thighs. Come to think of it, no one but him could have seen them, except for Nozomi. Shiori had to admit that Hinako was probably right.

Knowing this made it impossible for Shiori to engage with Suzuki-kun as she always had. If he was the source of the rumor, she needed to know why. What reason could he possibly have had for doing something so mean? Of course, she hoped more than anything that it would turn out to have been a misunderstanding.

She got her answer that same day, after school—though it took a while. She was so nervous that she kept beating around the bush for ages, managing to get to the point only in the evening. Still, eventually she bore down on the truth.

Suzuki-kun didn't deny it. He didn't even hesitate. But he also claimed that all he had done was mention the bruises, and that Hinako was the only one he had told. He had never said anything about Shiori being raped. He was so vehement about this that Shiori had no choice but to believe him.

And so she found herself without a clue who to believe. Scared of the truth, drained of her former spiritedness, she wanted to go home and cry herself to sleep.

The next day, however, when Hinako came over to talk to her just like always, Shiori was seized by the desire to hold her close, to ask her to explain. Desperate to believe in the purity of their friendship, she felt it was wrong of her to harbor even the slightest doubt.

Don't be fooled by Suzuki-kun, Hinako warned. He just wanted to push the blame onto someone else, to make himself seem innocent. He was a nasty character—he acted nice in front of Shiori so he could get what he wanted, but when she wasn't around, he said all kinds of awful things. Think of all the money he had borrowed. Had he ever paid her back for any of it? You couldn't trust anything a guy like that said.

Shiori was startled that Hinako's observations so closely echoed her sister's prediction, but that didn't make them any less persuasive. Now, finally, she saw Suzuki-kun for who he was. And yet somehow she remained torn, tugged in opposite directions by their competing claims. Unable to decide once and for all what was true, she shuttled back and forth between Suzuki-kun and Hinako, and so became even more isolated than before.

She didn't want either friendship to end. She had always been close with both of them, at least until she stayed home from school those few days. Her relationship with each of them had gotten a bit rocky, it was true, but as far as she could see it was all on account of that idiotic rumor, and she hoped things could still be repaired.

Even now, she couldn't quite confront reality.

Hinako was clearly the more trustworthy of the two. Suzuki-kun still hadn't repaid any of the money she had lent him, and, whether or not he had actually made up the rumor about her having been raped, he had admitted to telling Hinako about the bruises. If he hadn't done that, the rumor would never have started.

When she and Suzuki-kun were together, though, she didn't really get the sense that he was constantly making stuff up, and that left her as confused as ever. When she asked about the money, he got all indignant and started attacking *her*. That business about her cell phone being broken—that was all a lie, right? Once, he'd said he saw her talking to someone else, and he sounded so truly angry and jealous that she had begun to think, yet again, that he must really love her. Her own deep desire to be loved by him only strengthened this conviction, leaving her vision as clouded as ever, distancing her further from the reality of her situation.

Ultimately, it wasn't until Christmas Eve that the truth became clear to her.

She and Suzuki-kun were going to meet that evening. They hadn't planned a date, as most couples did; Suzuki-kun had told her at school on the last day before winter break that he was planning a Christmas party with some of his close friends. They were all going to chip in to rent out a café where one of his band members worked. It would be a small party, just friends and acquaintances, so Shiori said she would go.

Suzuki-kun seemed to be hoping this party would let him put his relationship with Shiori back on a good footing. At least, that was the impression she got when he suggested they could slip off and spend the rest of the night together when the rest of the group went off to continue the party somewhere else, as they inevitably would.

Shiori and Suzuki-kun had stopped spending time alone since their relationship had gone south, and she still wasn't sure she trusted him, but she was tempted by this proposal. She herself had been looking for some way to recapture the intimacy of their early days as a couple. And so, on Christmas Eve, Shiori decided to forget all that had happened between them and not worry about the future. She would go have fun at the party, enjoy being with Suzuki-kun. To an outside observer she might have seemed to be grasping at a spider's thread, pinning everything on the slenderest of hopes, but better that than sitting back and doing nothing. She wore a sundress she had ordered from a catalog, trying to make herself look as happy and as cute as possible, and then wrapped herself in an old Balenciaga coat she borrowed from her mother. That way she could surprise Suzuki-kun with the dress.

Soon after she left the house, Nozomi called. Her sister had gone out earlier with some high-school friends to a Christmas party organized by students at a nearby university. Shiori considered ignoring the call since she hadn't yet reached the bus stop and the bus was almost due, but picturing the consequences if Nozomi ever learned that she hadn't picked up when she was on her way to see Suzuki-kun persuaded her to answer.

Nozomi didn't say much, but her tone was domineering, as ever.

"Shiori, you need to come here right away."

Shiori said she couldn't, she was on her way to a party. But her protests fell on deaf ears. Nozomi didn't want any excuses, and besides, she insisted, Shiori wouldn't have to stay long. And so, just like that, Shiori gave in.

Fortunately, the café where Suzuki-kun and the rest were gathering wasn't far from where Nozomi was calling from, so Shiori probably wouldn't be too late, as long as whatever it was Nozomi wanted didn't take too long. Of course, knowing her sister and how egocentric she could be, it wasn't entirely inconceivable that Shiori would end up having some impossible task dumped on her, even on this joyful, sacred night. Perhaps for the time being it would be best not to mention Suzuki-kun, and just say she was going to a party with some classmates, leaving the tricky explanations for later.

Arriving outside the mixed-use building Nozomi had told her to come to, Shiori used the intercom to say she had arrived. She tried to keep optimistic, telling herself the supposedly urgent matter that had prompted her sister's call was probably something trivial—who knew, maybe she had a run in her stockings and wanted Shiori to go buy a new pair.

Having been directed to come up to the sixth floor, Shiori stepped into the sour-smelling, graffiti-covered elevator. She heard a low, regular thumping, the volume of which peaked at the fifth floor. When the elevator doors slid open and Shiori stepped out, five or six young men and women were standing in the hall with cigarettes and drinks in their hands. One of the young women who turned to look seemed to have been waiting for Shiori; gesturing toward a door down the hall, she said Nozomi was in there, in the office. As Shiori entered the room, she was startled to see a second familiar face beside her sister's. Before she could even say hello to her sister, she found herself gasping.

"Hinako! What happened?"

Hinako was crouched on the floor without her shoes on, her entire body soaking wet, as if someone had dumped a bucket of water over her head. Her eyes and lips were puffy, and her moss-green velour dress was torn and dirty. There was a dark patch on her chest that looked as though it could be blood.

Hinako maintained a sullen silence and stubbornly refused to make eye contact with Shiori, even as Shiori continued to ask, several times in succession, what had happened. She just went on rubbing her scratched kneecaps.

Shiori had no idea what to make of the sight of Hinako in this state, looking as if she had been subjected to some sort of violence, but even in her confusion the brutal air that hung in the room sent a chill down her spine. Unable to elicit a response from Hinako and having no idea what else to do, Shiori turned toward her sister, who sat in a chair ringed by her friends, like a boss with her gang. Nozomi, who until then had kept silent, regarding the scene with a detached eye, finally responded to her sister's questioning gaze.

"Now, Shiori, I want you to keep calm and listen to me. I'm going to give you some very important advice, OK? That's why I asked you here. From what I've been told, you're on your way to a party that guy is having. I would advise you not to go—not unless you want to end up like her."

Fragmentary visions of the various calamities that might have befallen Hinako flitted one after another through Shiori's mind.

"What happened?" Shiori asked again, addressing her sister this time.

A vision of an evil-looking Suzuki-kun rose up, unbidden in her mind, as her thoughts continued to race. With Hinako sitting there, looking as she did, Shiori had no other option but to keep silent and accept the reality confronting her.

"I should point out, first of all, that she really brought all this on herself. There's no need whatsoever for you to feel sorry for her. She got beaten up a little bit, and dragged around, but it's fine, it was nothing serious, OK? And *you* of all people have no reason to sympathize with her. That would be totally backwards. You're the one who should be hitting her, actually. I just roughed her up a bit beforehand, since you weren't here, and I happened to overhear her talking to some girls downstairs about things that were supposed to be kept secret from you—she got excited, you know, and let her voice get a bit too loud. Anyway, you're the one who should have done this."

Shiori felt very confused. All this was so different from what she had expected from her sister, and carried such unforeseen implications, that it took a while to grasp what it meant.

She tried to get some answers from Nozomi. *So it wasn't Suzuki-kun who left Hinako in this terrible state, it was you? Why would you want to do that? How is Suzuki-kun involved? How did you know I was going to Suzuki-kun's party tonight?*

Nozomi explained it all just as it had happened.

"You had no idea he was two-timing you, did you? She did, though, right from the start. She was bragging to her friends about it earlier, and she confessed to me, so there's no doubt about it—she's dating him. I wouldn't even call it two-timing; he was just exploiting you. She's his real girlfriend, and he only pretended you two were dating to get money out of you. Of course, that's how she described it, so he may actually see you *both* as total pushovers who'll do whatever he says. It wouldn't surprise me if that were the case. In any event, you get it now, right? He's trash, that guy, like I've been saying all along. He's worse than worthless, tricking you, of all people, not giving a shit, and getting it on with this piece of trash, making fun of you behind your back the whole time, telling people you're tone deaf and slow and whatever—absolute garbage. I hear everyone at school is saying you've been raped. You know who started that rumor? Little what's-her-name here, this loose little bitch. She's desperate to hold on to that guy, to keep him for herself, so evidently she's been bad-mouthing you to him right from the start. The girls she was with earlier testified to that. Seems he started going around with you first, so maybe she was worried. She thought she might end up in your place, and you'd take hers—and sure, it's true, it could have happened at any moment. She saw her chance when you stopped coming to school, so she spread that rumor. She thought he'd want to keep his distance from you if there was talk about you being raped. It's hilarious, huh? Why do idiots like her always come up with such bad ideas? Honestly, I was kind of impressed at how bad it was. And speaking of being raped, if you go to that Christmas party, that's exactly what's going to happen—the rumor will come true. So you're going to go straight home, you hear? It seems that was his plan all along—that's the whole reason he organized this party, because he knew you'd fall for it. He'd get you drunk, and they'd all do it together. Guys like him do this sort of thing all the time. Just what you'd expect from these barbarians. If you don't believe me, Shiori darling, just ask her. He told her everything."

Shiori cast a nervous, sideways glace at Hinako. Their eyes met, but Hinako averted her gaze before it started to feel like she had to speak.

"Hinako?" Shiori called quietly, suppressing her emotions. But still Hinako said nothing. Shiori felt as if she were facing a stranger. Too exhausted and dispirited to keep pushing for a reply, she simply sighed.

They seemed to have reached a stalemate, with no one prepared to say anything, when all of a sudden a girl from Nozomi's gang stalked angrily over to Hinako and directed a rough kick at her back, barking that she should answer when she was spoken to.

Hinako tumbled forward, ending up hunched over with her hands on the floor. Scared that another kick might follow, she immediately curled up and darted to one side even as she burst into a coughing fit. When the first girl raised her foot again, Hinako instinctively moved to defend herself, putting her arms up around her head, and blurted out that it was all true. Clearly, she didn't like having to admit it, but she had no choice.

By the time Hinako turned to look at Shiori, she had stopped trying to conceal her malice; her eyes brimmed with spite. Now it was Shiori's turn to wish she could flee, and she turned away to escape Hinako's gaze.

The silence continued as the office door opened and a young man poked his head in from the hallway. "Still going?" he asked, to which Nozomi replied curtly that they would be done in a moment. The man nodded and disappeared back into the hall, letting the door close on its own.

"At any rate, you really got lucky, Shiori. Don't you think? I'm sure you're happy to have escaped the danger. You wasted three months with that guy before you figured out what he's like, but it all worked out at the last moment, and now you're safe. All's well that ends well, right? Try to see it that way. In that sense, it's great for us that this girl can't control herself and blabs the way she does. There's good karma there, too. Sucks for her that your sister just happened to be listening when she was talking crap about you. It's nice to have such a caring kid sister, huh? I can't always be looking out for you, though, Shiori, so you're going to have to get better at sizing people up. It's time you grew up a bit, don't you think?"

Nozomi looked like an angel in her white chiffon dress, but her tone was so full of malice that it made Shiori a bit uneasy. Everything her sister had said was true, of course, and yet it almost seemed to Shiori that Nozomi wasn't really on her side—a result, perhaps, of the harsh, derisive attitude that had become Nozomi's default. It struck Shiori that her sister wasn't doing herself any favors by acting like this, and she decided to tell her this the next day. Worrying about her sister was the only way Shiori could distract herself from the painful truth confronting her.

So it came about that Shiori stopped dating Suzuki-kun.

Shiori herself never said anything to him, but, sometime over winter break, Hinako seemed to have told him what happened on Christmas Eve. Suzuki-kun, for his part, never even tried to justify himself. He never gave back the money he owed her, either, or made any excuses for not doing so—he just ignored her, refusing all contact. No one in Shiori's circle ever mentioned their relationship, or seemed puzzled that it had ended, so it was almost as if it had all been in Shiori's mind.

This was true of her friendship with Hinako, as well. From the time they started twelfth grade in April until they graduated a year later, Hinako treated Shiori the same way Suzuki-kun did, acting as if they were total strangers. Hinako never said anything about the violence she had suffered on Christmas Eve, either. It wasn't something she wanted to remember.

As if to make up for her loss of these two relationships, former friends who had drifted away from her began, little by little over the days and months, to enter Shiori's life again. She never grew so close with these people that they would meet up on weekends, for instance, but Shiori was still glad to have people to talk to at school. Over time, her interactions with these others helped her feel less isolated, though she often found herself thinking that a poet's lot really was a lonely one.

●

The spring after her high school graduation, Shiori moved to Tokyo to study songwriting at a music school. The entrance exam, which took place in December, consisted of two simple written tests in music and Japanese language, as well as a brief interview. Shiori was terrified that they would ask her to sing during the interview, but that didn't happen; a week after the test, she received a notice informing her that she had been accepted.

Though her new environment allowed her to devote herself to her songs, Shiori still felt as depressed as before. She had left home eager to push bravely on toward her dreams, but there were hurdles everywhere. In fact, reality would soon pummel her with a cruelty beyond anything she had experienced before.

Her life in Tokyo remained solitary. It was exhilarating to be in the city, teeming as it was with new experiences, even if some involved making a mess of unfamiliar household tasks, and, each time she left her apartment, she encountered new scenery, which kept her from ever growing bored. Ever the optimist, Shiori couldn't wait to make new friends at school and looked forward to talking with others who shared her dreams.

The one-room apartment she had rented in Sangenjaya, Setagaya-ku, was the perfect place to lose herself in writing lyrics, and in fantasizing about the future. A nearby shopping arcade had a club that did live shows and a rehearsal studio, so every time she went shopping she would see fans who had lined up to see whatever band would be playing, or even guitar-case-carrying musicians. The sight of all these people made her feel like she had stumbled upon a convention of modern troubadours, and she wished so badly that she could join them, talk with them—but she lacked the courage. Instead, she would go back to her apartment and imagine that she was in a band, chatting with imaginary fans, or see her future self giving advice to the young woman who would be singing her songs.

She didn't have much luck making friends at school. A number of the students in the songwriting track hit it off within the first day or two, and by the end of the first week the class had split into a few groups whose members did everything together. Shiori didn't wind up in any of these, so she often went through an entire day without exchanging a word with anyone. She never tried to join the conversations going on around her, and no one else came over to talk to her... and then the day was over, and it was time to go home. She had become noticeably more timid than when she lived in the countryside.

There was a reason for this. On the first day, one of their teachers had asked everyone to sing a bit of a favorite song as a lead-in to introducing themselves. He always asked students to do this, he explained—it was a nice way to get acquainted at a music school. And so, right after she enrolled, she was struck by her first catastrophe, which put a wedge between her and her classmates. As a way of atoning for her role in the death of those parakeets, she had forbidden herself to sing in public, and she wasn't about to break that vow to accommodate some school convention. She kept hemming and hawing, despite her teacher's increasingly irate attempts to cajole her, and the rest of the students began to lose the excitement they had been feeling and turned one after the other to glare at her.

When the teacher demanded an explanation and she replied that she was unbelievably tone deaf, all the other students burst out laughing. Some wondered aloud how someone like that had gotten into music school. Faced with this new student who looked so timid and yet absolutely refused to give in, the teacher looked like he wanted to march over and slap her. And yet, even the sight of him quaking with rage—a narrow-minded, hot-blooded hulk, more like a gym teacher than a musician—didn't sway Shiori; she simply sat in her seat with tears in her eyes, clenching her teeth.

Shiori's refusal to sing derailed the class so badly that they had to postpone her self-introduction. The teacher said he didn't want to see her speaking to any of the other students until she agreed to sing. He must have assumed she would give in after being told off like this, but it had no effect. Indeed, for a time she took his injunction seriously and didn't say a word at school. She accepted this punishment as yet another hardship she had to endure in atonement for the evil she had done.

Only after another teacher released her from this inter-diction on speaking—having a mute in class got in the way of his teaching, he said—did she begin communicating with the other students in her track. But by then it was too late: she had missed her chance to form genuine friendships. The students had finished sorting themselves, and it was all but impossible for a young woman as awkward as her to get past the many walls that had been thrown up around her and get to know her classmates. The bad impression she had made on the first day, and the fact that, ultimately, she never got the chance to introduce herself, only compounded her difficulties. Her teacher made no secret of his animosity, refusing to have anything to do with her even during class.

Thus, though she was never bored, Shiori found herself living a very lonely life in the city, and by mid-April she was already feeling rather homesick. She almost burst out crying one day when Nozomi suddenly informed her over the phone that her parents weren't going to let her come home during the Golden Week vacation, and in fact she did emit a sort of yelp. Suspecting this was really just another random prohibition by her younger sister, Shiori asked to speak to their mother, only to learn that it was true—her father's restaurant chain was going through a rough patch, this wasn't a good time, and it would be best if she stayed away. So, it wasn't just Nozomi being mean after all. Her mother didn't want to worry Shiori with the details, it wasn't all that big a deal, but it would be a real help if she could sit tight until summer vacation. In the end, Shiori agreed not to go home during the break.

Lonelier than ever, and with her only escape route blocked, Shiori finally hit upon a way to assuage the hunger for communication that plagued her throughout Golden Week: an online forum for "email buddies" that she could access through her cell phone. She wasn't terribly eager to meet anyone in person, but she did want to have some sort of relationship, even if it was limited to casual exchanges over email.

Shiori began emailing back and forth fairly frequently with two of her new online friends. The exchanges continued even after the break ended; as time went by, Shiori began writing more often. She began to feel less lonely than before. In reality, she was still just as alone as before, but it didn't bother her so much.

One of her new email buddies was a sickly boy, evidently two or three years younger than her, who used the handle

"Z." He had mentioned in one of his emails that he was stuck at home—he'd had to take a leave from high school from the spring, shortly after he moved up to the next grade, to concentrate on his recovery.

Surprisingly enough, the second friend she had made was a foreigner—a Portuguese man about ten years her senior who had been living in Japan for eight years. His name was Manuel, and he played drums in a rock band with three Japanese university students.

Shiori had answered a number of other friend requests on the same forum, and a few of the people had even replied; but only these two responded regularly to her communications, offering their thoughts about any topic Shiori broached. Though she had only made two of these friends, she loved being able to write to them whenever she wanted, and she took to emailing them numerous times a day.

Most of her messages were about little things that had happened in the course of her day. But at night, as she sat staring blankly at her television, she would open up to her two friends about her most private thoughts and anxieties. They would write back with questions, which she would answer honestly, so that over time she came to feel a deep desire to have them know her as she really was, and she began writing completely candidly about her childhood and where she came from, holding nothing back. She shared everything: her dream of becoming a troubadour, and how she had given up; her new plan to become a lyricist; how isolated she had felt in middle school, and then in high school; all the things that had gone wrong with her love life, and with her friends. She talked about her family; about the death of the parakeets, and her culpability; and about the troubles she was having at school.

Day after day, she wrote about these things in the messages she sent off to her two email buddies. Sometimes, as her thumb danced across the buttons of her cell phone, she would feel as though she were composing her autobiography. Without her realizing it, sending out these late-night confessions had become an important element of her daily routine.

●

Manuel was the first to suggest they get together in person. Not that he asked her out on a date or anything like that; he invited her to come see his band. Shiori was thrilled.

The band played only about twenty minutes, but Shiori, easily moved as ever, stood dazed for a while after the set ended, her hands, once she stopped applauding, clasped in front of her. The songs had been so intense that she couldn't make out the lyrics, which was unfortunate—though it was also possible, she thought, that Manuel had intended to leave people wanting to hear more, and, if so, that was an entirely natural approach. In any event, she was deeply happy to have met a group of genuine troubadours.

The show had taken place in the live house near her apartment, a fact that made her feel connected to Manuel and the band's other members in a way she hadn't anticipated. It was as if her wish had been granted—the wish that rose up inside her each time she walked past that venue, that she might join the troubadours who gathered there. This helped her forget, for a time, the loneliness of school. More than anything, she was grateful to Manuel for that.

Though his writing lacked a certain polish, she hadn't felt when she read Manuel's emails that she was communicating with someone Portuguese. This came home to her when they finally met face-to-face. His swarthy skin and chiseled features; his full black hair and thick eyebrows; and his bright, expansive manner all coincided almost perfectly with her stereotype of a member of the Latin races.

Shiori knew nothing at all about Portugal, and when she had a chance to talk to Manuel in person for the first time, she decided she ought to start studying up on it. She realized with chagrin that her exchanges with Manuel and Z had all been centered on her own issues, and she knew next to nothing about their lives.

Shiori ended up joining the after-party, where Manuel introduced her to the rest of the band, calling them by their given names: Tsugumi was the vocalist; Kuniko played the guitar; Tetsuya was on bass. They were all at the same university, and one year older than Shiori.

For much of the party, Shiori simply sat with her mouth

agape, unable to keep up with the conversation—it was her first time meeting everyone, after all, and there was a lot of talk about school and other bands. Still, she overcame her timidity enough to strike up conversations with Tsugumi and Kuniko, and she exchanged phone numbers and email addresses not just with them, but also with Tetsuya. When she told Tetsuya she lived nearby, he remarked pleasantly that it was cool to be so close. As the party ended, Tsugumi, the band's leader, promised to let her know when they booked their next gig. Walking back to her apartment in the dark, Shiori felt happy for the first time in ages.

April had been a pretty rough month, all in all, but since her luck seemed to have turned in May—not only had she made new acquaintances, she had even been admitted into a circle of troubadours!—she no longer felt lonely as often as she did at school, where she still had no one to talk to. She owed this, too, to Manuel and Z, and she made sure to send each of them an email saying how grateful she was.

Manuel sent a gentlemanly reply saying he had done nothing to deserve her gratitude and thanking her for coming to hear the band. Z's email had a slightly different tone. Overall, it was a nice message, but he also warned her to be careful:

> I hate to be a downer, but I don't think you ought to be too trusting. Not if you don't want to mess things up with people like you did in high school.

Z's reaction seemed a lot like what she would expect from her sister, and this got her thinking about the life he was living. Maybe it hadn't been very thoughtful of her to send him a giddy email about how happy she was to have made new friends when he was bedridden, unable to go out and meet anyone face to face. It wasn't a good way to show him how grateful she was to him. In fact, it was insensitive.

Now that she *had* considered his perspective, though, she didn't think it would be wise to send an apologetic email or make excuses for what she had done. She just thanked him for his advice and went to bed, her thoughts filled, as she drifted off, with self-loathing.

Shiori was so focused on trying to understand Z's feelings that she completely forgot the advice he had given her and made no effort to be more cautious or vigilant in managing her relationships. Maybe if she had heeded Z's warning, a different path would have opened up before her. Because in the end, his fears turned out to be right on target.

●

Shiori was busy all June: and then it was July. On weekdays she attended classes at school and worked from early evening until late at night at a family restaurant. She did shifts at the restaurant on weekends, too, and during her break she would call Tsugumi to ask if there were any tasks she could take care of after work. Even when Shiori didn't call, Tsugumi was constantly emailing with chores she wanted done, so Shiori had to keep on her toes all day, morning to night. Tsugumi lived alone in an apartment one train station away, and she would sometimes take advantage of their proximity, summoning Shiori in the middle of the night to have her pick up a few items at a convenience store or discount shop. This had continued without interruption throughout the entire month of June.

The reason Shiori was so busy was that she had agreed to serve as the band's manager. This sounded impressive, but in reality she just did whatever little things needed doing; over time, it came to seem increasingly like she was Tsugumi's personal servant.

Tsugumi really liked Shiori. Evidently, she had been pushing the other band members to let Shiori join ever since they had first met at that after-party. Manuel had written to her about that. Shiori replied immediately that while she was truly honored, she didn't think she would be of much use since she was unbelievably tone deaf and couldn't play any instruments. Ten minutes later, she was startled to receive a phone call from Tsugumi herself. According to Tsugumi, the band had been practicing in a rehearsal studio until half an hour ago, and afterward they'd had a meeting, and Shiori came up. As a matter of fact, they were in a coffee shop near the live house right now—could Shiori join them? The invitation pleased Shiori, of course, and she went out right away.

When she arrived, Shiori told everyone once again that she was sorry, but she couldn't accept their invitation. Basically, the only time she had ever laid hands on a musical instrument was when she played her recorder in music class in elementary and middle school, so she honestly wasn't qualified to be in a band, she would only get in the way. She really regretted that this was the case, but she simply couldn't do it.

Unfazed, Tsugumi kept trying to persuade Shiori to join in one capacity or another—anything, it didn't matter what it was. She kept at it with striking persistence, as if she knew Shiori would eventually give in and accept. Shiori, for her part, could think of no appropriate response other than to cock her head, hold out her hands, and groan in a manner suggestive of how torn she felt, even though she looked distinctly delighted. No one had ever needed her as badly as these people did, she could see that, and deep down she really wanted to tell them how happy their need for her made her feel. She was a bit bewildered by the fact that her own hang-ups kept her from doing this.

Manuel must have felt sorry for Shiori, seeing her so torn and confused, because when the long back-and-forth about her joining the band finally ended in a draw, he suggested that if she didn't feel she could be a full-fledged member, maybe she could sign on as manager. He must have remembered, from her emails, that she had helped out with Suzuki-kun's band in the fall of her second year in high school.

This seemed like a good compromise. Shiori had said she wanted to be involved in one way or another, even if being a member wasn't realistic, and since all Tsugumi wanted was to connect Shiori to the band, she couldn't very well object to Manuel's plan, either.

Far from making Shiori happy, though, this compromise would turn out to have been a sort of trap, because the thing that drew Tsugumi to Shiori was not her musical sensibilities, but the fact that she was so obliging and so easy with her money. Tsugumi had instantly recognized Shiori as one of those young women who just can't say no, who would accede to any request as long as it was aggressive enough. Tsugumi also appeared to have gleaned as much information about Shiori as she could from Manuel, and among the things she had learned was the history of Shiori's relationship with Suzuki-kun.

Shiori was unaware of this, so Tsugumi could manipulate her as she pleased, persuading Shiori to open her wallet just as liberally as she had for Suzuki-kun. Now that Shiori was their manager, Tsugumi proposed that they start settling the band's expenses at the end of each month, with Shiori covering all of the costs in the meantime. This put a substantial burden on Shiori, even if she was going to be paid back—for an amateur band that hadn't even released an album yet, the group used quite a lot of money. Shiori covered everything from rental fees for the rehearsal studio to the food and drink consumed during meetings and the bills for various accessories for their instruments. She even ended up going along to shop for clothes that were supposedly meant to be worn on stage or heading out in the middle of the night to buy household supplies, liquor and magazines.

All this led to a precipitous decline in Shiori's savings, to the extent that she had to ask her mother for an advance on her monthly allowance. Her mother consented but said she wouldn't be able to do this again—the family's finances weren't so great right now. This left Shiori with no option, as she tried to think how she could come up with additional funds in the future, but to go out and earn more money on her own.

Since she had agreed to be manager without having any notion what was entailed, she ended up saying yes to every request, and worked like crazy. It would have been reasonable for her to complain, since the band wasn't successful enough to need a manager, and especially given the outrageous demands Tsugumi was always making, but Shiori felt so giddy at having been admitted into a group of troubadours that she didn't see things this way and tried her best to be useful. She was so busy trying to keep track of all the money she was spending that she didn't even have the energy to nurture suspicions of Tsugumi.

Tsugumi wasn't the only band member eager to sponge off Shiori, either. Tetsuya was especially bad, in part because he took a different approach, more cunning and depraved than Tsugumi's headlong rush to exploit Shiori. Tetsuya was constantly on the lookout for moments when he could get Shiori alone, so he could start letting on that he was interested in her.

Tetsuya first tested this strategy the day after Tsugumi dragged Shiori off on a trip to buy "stage clothes." If Shiori had been capable of sizing him up objectively, she would have been shocked at his brazenness, but, at such times, thinking rationally was beyond her. She had been burned by Suzuki-kun once before, yes, but she couldn't help being pleased when men appeared to be attracted to her, and she didn't try to push Tetsuya away. She figured it would take a while for her to develop feelings for him—they had only just met each other, after all, and she had never regarded him as a potential boyfriend—and yet if he were to come out and confess that he liked her, she felt she would have to think seriously about their relationship.

She couldn't stand the thought of anyone disliking her, and she really didn't want to have problems with anyone in the band. She resigned herself to accommodating their requests as best she could, or even a little more. Tetsuya sensed this—and exploited it.

The last Sunday in June, Shiori woke up at eight so she could work the entire morning. She watched TV while having her usual warm sandwich for breakfast. Shiori loved warm sandwiches; she had asked her parents to buy her a sandwich toaster when she moved to Tokyo. Every morning, she fixed herself a sandwich with ham, cheese, and thinly sliced onions.

She had the sandwich with a glass of tomato juice and a cup of lactoferrin-rich yogurt.

When her morning anime ended, she went and brushed her teeth. She was still brushing when her cell phone rang, so she quickly wiped her mouth with a towel and ran over to her phone. By the time she got it, the ringing had stopped.

It had been Tetsuya. It seemed odd that he had called so early, so she called him back. He told her he had to see her today, he just had to, no matter what.

There was a news program on the TV now. A white-haired newscaster was standing in front of the White House reading out his report. He carried on at length about a significant advance in peace negotiations between the United States–Israel alliance and the Islamic nations of the Middle East, noting that, despite continued resistance from extremist groups, it seemed increasingly likely that the turmoil that had characterized international relations in the decade since 9/11 might finally be drawing to an end, and that a final agreement would indeed be forthcoming. As soon as he had said his piece, the camera cut back to the TV studio, and a panel of scholars and journalists launched into a discussion of this new development.

Shiori told Tetsuya she could see him after work. She noted down the meeting place and hung up. Then she grabbed the remote to check the weather and begin preparing to go out.

Her eye was drawn to a headline running across the bottom of the screen: "Multiple cases of bird flu confirmed in domestic poultry farms." Her heart ached at these words. She thought of all the birds who would die, and her eyes grew moist. Inevitably, her mind turned to the parakeets at the pet shop who had passed away in her second year of high school.

At seven that evening, Shiori went to meet Tetsuya in Shibuya. He took her to a music store where he had found an electric bass he really wanted; the store had been holding it for him since yesterday. Her mind blank from exhaustion after a long day waiting tables, Shiori stood in a corner of the store while Tetsuya chatted with the clerk he had asked for help. Never before had she felt the need to work as hard as she did these days, or study so intensely for school, and she was utterly worn out. Now that she no longer had to stay focused the way she did when she was on the job, her brain had stopped functioning altogether, leaving her a bit confused about what she was doing in this store in the first place. She came to when someone called her name, then tapped her on the shoulder. OK, Tetsuya announced, she could pay now—everything was ready. Shiori glanced at the paper the clerk held out to her and saw the figure: "¥487,200, tax included." She gasped audibly.

Tetsuya and the clerk stared at her, annoyed that she was taking so long.

"Uh... well..." she stammered, fumbling for her wallet. But all she had with her was ¥13,865—not enough, obviously, to cover ¥487,200, tax included.

"I don't know if..." Shiori mumbled.

Tetsuya came up and threw his arm around her shoulder.

"It's OK," he murmured into her ear. "You can pay by credit card."

She did have one credit card in her wallet. It was the family card—her parents had added her name to the account when she moved to Tokyo. It was her policy to use it only when she really needed to, in emergencies, so she wouldn't waste money, and she was hesitant to hand it over to the clerk. But when Tetsuya urged her with a friendly smile to hurry so they could go get something to eat, she decided maybe it wasn't such a big deal. It was almost the end of the month, she thought optimistically; the money would come back almost immediately.

Fortunately for Tetsuya, Shiori hadn't used the card at all that month, so the charge didn't push her over the limit. As she watched him take the bass in its hard case from the clerk, a satisfied grin on his face, Shiori told herself it was all for the best. Though even then she felt a nervous fluttering in her chest.

At the end of the month, when the time came for everyone to repay her, Manuel was the only one who gave her exactly what he owed. Kuniko wasn't too bad, either: she coughed up half of the total. Tetsuya and Tsugumi just made excuses. According to Tetsuya, the sensible thing was for him to pay her back on the credit card's billing date, since there might be other charges, too. Tsugumi apologized in a rather cloying manner, then said she didn't see how she could have spent so much, and that she would just have to be in Shiori's debt for a while because her parents weren't sending her anything these days and she didn't have enough to cover even basic expenses.

Still, it never even occurred to Shiori that Tsugumi might have no intention of paying her back. She was somewhat skeptical when it came to Tetsuya, but she decided to give him the benefit of the doubt. Maybe she was being ridiculously naive, but she didn't want to ruin things with Tsugumi and Tetsuya and lose her position as manager. Even if she ended up regretting it, for the time being she was happier playing along than she would be if she had to go back to being all alone again.

●

At school, Shiori remained as isolated as ever. The minute classes ended, she always headed off to the restaurant where she worked, and, whenever she had time off school, she spent the whole day either waiting tables or dashing around, taking care of odd jobs for the band, so she never had much of a chance to get to know her classmates.

She didn't really feel comfortable in any of her classes, either. There was a good reason for this: she couldn't compose any lyrics. She had always had difficulty writing, whether she was working on a poem or a song. This had been the case ever since middle school, when she first committed to the troubadour life, but until she enrolled in this school with the express goal of studying lyric-writing, she had never understood why she had such trouble. Once her lyric-writing program got underway, she realized that in her mind lyrics really had to be sung—that was how they were meant to be experienced. Lyrics came into being as an expression of the voice, not as marks on paper, which failed to convey the subtle nuances of each tiny sound in each individual word, and were thus imprecise, unable to communicate feelings with the necessary clarity.

The more time she spent in school, the more settled this conviction became. As a result, she had been unable to compose even a single lyric on any of the topics her instructors gave out, and their views of her grew even dimmer than before. They had been urging her to turn in at least one or two finished lyrics by summer vacation, but she was afraid she wasn't going to be able to do it.

When she wrote to Z and Manuel to ask their thoughts about all this, they gave contradictory advice. In Z's view, learning to write lyrics wasn't really any different from learning to write essays—grasping certain common techniques was sure to prove useful. He suggested she try and look at things differently, to think of lyrics in their written form as an entirely different type of expression and see if she could produce anything that way. Manuel, in contrast, said he thought she was one-hundred-percent right: lyrics were meant to be vocalized, and she should stand by her convictions. He proposed that she try improvising for her instructors, performing her lyrics as a sort of rap. She had to make them understand that her lyrics had to be voiced, that's just how it was.

Shiori was inclined to take Manuel's advice, but since she had forbidden herself ever to sing, she could follow it only halfway. The thought of granting herself a temporary reprieve did occur to her, of course—it was an assignment, after all—but she knew her voice wouldn't sound the way she wanted it to, even if she tried to sing. Her body would refuse to play along, no matter how much she wanted to sing. In any event, she had forgotten how.

On the morning of Friday, July 1, twenty-two days before the start of summer vacation, Shiori went to school with an idea in mind. She was going to perform for her instructor.

A surprisingly simple shift in perspective had helped her reclaim her optimism.

Rereading Manuel's message with Z's advice in mind had given her the hint she needed. Changing her thinking just a bit would enable her to follow Manuel's suggestion. Since singing was the problem, all she had to do was drop the melody, speak the lyrics in her normal voice.

For some reason, though, classes seemed to have been canceled that day. An hour after school was supposed to start, the students still couldn't get into the building. Some decided to treat this as a day off and left; others waited patiently outside for someone from school to arrive. Shiori, eager to present her response to the assignment, joined those waiting.

Though the rainy season hadn't yet officially ended, the day was clear and summery, and the temperature was climbing rapidly. There was a limit to how long students would be able to wait outside. Fortunately, two members of the student-affairs staff turned up shortly before noon. Rather than open the building, however, they announced that unforeseen circumstances had made it necessary for the school to close temporarily, and that classes would continue as usual on the following Monday. They taped a note saying the same thing to the door and then left immediately.

Shiori was stunned, having lost the only outlet she had for her newfound drive almost as soon as she had discovered it. Still in a daze, she went back home. She had no other choice.

That evening, plagued with anxiety about whether she could rekindle the eagerness she'd felt that morning when she returned to school next Monday, she nonetheless did her best to keep smiling as she interacted with diners during her shift at the restaurant.

On Saturday, she waited tables from morning until the early afternoon before joining the band for an evening rehearsal. That night, they went and had a meeting over dinner at the restaurant where Shiori worked. Shiori had hoped the three members who hadn't yet paid her back would do so at this meeting, but that didn't happen.

On Sunday, Shiori worked all day, from morning until night. She had originally planned to leave at five, but one of the other part-timers called in sick and the manager asked her to work overtime to fill in.

It wasn't until just after ten that she realized she had an email from Tsugumi asking her to drop by after work. This was unfortunate. The thought that she had kept Tsugumi waiting for five hours made Shiori break out in a cold sweat. She called immediately, only to be told, in a tone of undisguised irritation, that she was no longer needed. All she could do was offer a nervous apology.

Worrying that Tsugumi might be getting fed up with her made Shiori feel a bit depressed, and by the time she got back to her apartment she felt utterly drained. There was bad news waiting for her when she arrived. Very bad news indeed.

Shiori hadn't spoken to her family for three weeks, and the last time they had called, she and her mother had talked for only a few minutes. Her mother had told her then, speaking quietly and in an even tone, that since her father's business still hadn't gotten back on track, starting the next month they would no longer be able to send any money. Until the family's finances improved, Shiori would have to look after herself, paying her way with her job.

"I'm sorry, Shiori—sorry that you must suffer on our account."

Hearing her mother murmur lines straight out of an old TV drama, Shiori felt her chest tighten. She tried to sound as cheerful as possible, assuring her mother with feigned optimism that everything would be OK, hoping it wouldn't be obvious how distressed she really was. Only after she hung up did she allow herself to cry silently.

Tonight, three weeks later, it was Nozomi who called to deliver the unfortunate news that their father's business had gone under. In recent years, the large *yakitori* chain he ran across southern Tōhoku had been forced, little by little, to retrench. Basically, the company had failed to react quickly enough to declining demand—a problem that stemmed from a culture of poor management that had emerged when times were good, as people got used to thinking big, making investments that, in retrospect, had been too bold. This had hurt their cash flow, and then, to make matters worse, some of the poultry farms they worked with had lost literally all their chickens to bird flu. Other farms were facing the same problem, of course, so there was nowhere they could turn to get the meat they needed. Ultimately, they were forced to shut down the entire chain for a while, twice making it impossible for the company to meet its creditors' deadlines, and now they were essentially bankrupt.

"So that's the situation, Shiori. We can't go on living as we have been. It's awful, I know, but there's nothing we can do. We won't be able to keep this wonderful house, either—we'll have to let it go—it and all the precious memories it holds. It's incredibly painful, it cuts just thinking of it. Mom feels awful that she didn't let you come home for Golden Week, seeing how things have turned out. Don't hold it against them, though, Shiori. They're both totally exhausted from all this. You'd be shocked to see how thin they are now, and the big bags under their eyes. They've hardly slept for days on end. Dad had to meet with the creditors yesterday, and since he's the face of the company they were all blaming him, saying terrible things about his management. He said they were cursing. Cursing him out so badly he wished he could just curl up and die—can you imagine that? Dad, who's always been so strong. And Mom's taking it even worse. She's in shock that Auntie wouldn't help out with any money. She's always grousing about how different things would have been if Grandpa were still alive. Mom and Auntie never really got along, of course. So we can't count on getting anything from Grandpa's old clinic. Dad wants to skip town, to run out on the creditors... It's too early to say what will happen, though. In any event, don't worry about me, Shiori. I'll get along somehow. I'll go my own way. Apparently, Auntie was kind enough to say she'd look after the two of us—Mom told me. I don't need her help, though. I've decided to drop out of high school. I don't see much point spending three years there. Honestly, you come out stupider than when you went in. Everything they teach you is pointless, really. A waste of time. I'll be able to make it on my own. I'll be OK, whatever happens. I'm more concerned about you, Shiori. It's going to be hard. Auntie says she'll take care of your tuition, but it sounds like you'll have to cover your living expenses..."

After her sister shared all this, Shiori talked with her parents. She and her mother couldn't have much of a conversation, since neither of them could hide their tears; when she told her father she was going to withdraw from school the next day and go straight home, he asked her not to be rash, since there was no knowing how things might develop.

For the time being, he would be going over their debts and assets, trying to arrange things, but they might need to go off somewhere far away with very little warning. Given the fluid, precarious state things were in, it would be best if she stayed in Tokyo and continued her studies until they had figured out what they were doing on their end. He understood how she felt, of course, but for now it would be wisest for them not to have any contact with her at all—he hoped she would see that this was necessary and endure it.

Her father's tone made it clear this was an order, so she couldn't protest. She told him, through her tears, that she understood.

It was almost dawn by the time this long, long phone call ended. Shiori thought about going to bed after she placed her phone in the charger, but she didn't; she sat listlessly on the floor, slumped against the wall, thinking back over her eighteen years in the house where she had been born and raised. She cried so much that she ran out of tissues.

She was still sitting in the same spot when her alarm clock suddenly started chirping, its cheerful tone utterly out of place. Somehow it was time to start getting ready for school.

She had the impression her sentimental trip down memory lane had lasted ten minutes at most and was dumbstruck to realize that hours had passed.

Obeying her father, she took the subway to school.

Lack of sleep made her eyelids look even puffier than they usually would after she had cried, but she didn't care. This was no time to fret over trivialities—not when her parents and her sister were going through so much. She would go wait tables at the restaurant in the evening, and afterward she would look in at the rehearsal studio and help the band. She could apologize to Tsugumi for missing her yesterday, too. By carrying on with her life as usual, she could give her family one less thing to worry about—that, she told herself, was her duty. It was all she *could* do. This realization made her feel newly powerless, but she fought hard not to let it get to her.

Reality had even more in store for Shiori, however. Exiting the station and walking down the street toward school, she found herself confronting precisely the same scene she had encountered on Friday morning. Once again, there was a crowd of students outside the door to the building, unable to get in. The only difference was that the note saying classes had been canceled had already been posted. One got the sense that there would be no school the following day, either, or the day after that. According to the note, the school had been closed because members of the board, including the chairman and vice chairman, were suspected of having embezzled funds. A teacher who had acted as a whistleblower had been fired, and this led the rest of the faculty, who had been increasingly at odds with the administration over the school's management, to refuse to work, making it impossible for the school to function.

The students were clearly agitated. This time, very few wandered off, happy to get a day off: some simply hung around, looking lost, while others discussed how the situation might develop, their faces grave.

Eventually, the two student-affairs staff members showed up again, this time to take down the notice. They seemed utterly indifferent. Seeing them, the students gathered outside the building grew more agitated. When a few students demanded to be told why they were removing the notice, one of the staff explained that they didn't want students to be misled—the school was just closed another day, that was all. They gave no explanation for the closure, and were obviously interested only in getting away, even if they left people more confused than before. A wave of discontent radiated out through the crowd. The two staff members, completely encircled, tried to excuse themselves, saying they would share information about future classes as it became available, but by then the students were in no mood for games. They began calling for the chairman and the other board members to come out, in response to which the two staff just folded their arms and shook their heads. Things were coming to a head.

Shiori, having worked from morning until night the day before and then gotten no sleep, started feeling so ill from the burning sun and the crowds that even crouching down didn't help. Incapable of staying longer to see how the situation would develop, she decided to return to her apartment.

Back at home, she collapsed on her futon without undressing and almost immediately drifted off. When she woke it was pitch black, leading her for a moment to think she had somehow wandered into the afterworld. Her whole body was clammy with sweat; she felt weighed down by thirst and hunger; and she had a disagreeable sensation in her mouth. As her eyes adjusted to the darkness, she saw that it was black outside, too, past the curtains. With an ache like heartburn in her chest, she reached over, switched on the lights and glanced at the clock. It was 7:30 p.m. The biggest crunch time at the restaurant where she worked.

●

Shiori called the restaurant and told the manager honestly that she had overslept, and that she was sorry. He very generously said he would overlook it this time, but only this once. The college student who had gotten sick and stayed home the day before had taken Shiori's place. Everything had sort of balanced out, but Shiori still felt terrible for having come perilously close to missing the start of her shift without even calling in, inconveniencing a coworker and her manager. She couldn't ever let this happen again. Now that she wasn't getting any money from her parents, she really couldn't afford to lose her job.

Still, the manager had enough waiters on hand, and the other girl said she wouldn't need to stay much longer anyway, so Shiori decided to take the evening off. The band wouldn't get started in the studio until nine, so she had time to shower and have something to eat. She decided she would aim to finish dinner by eight-thirty, then set out a bit early so she could be waiting for everyone at the studio when they arrived.

When she arrived at the studio, she started heading up to the second-floor lobby to sign in. As she reached the landing, she heard two familiar voices, one male and one female, coming from the top of the stairs. For the first time in a long time, her heart leapt. It felt so good to be back with friends that she started to dash up the last flight of stairs, only to freeze in place after just two steps. Her friends were talking about her, she realized. What they were saying wasn't very nice.

"I think it's time we ditched her. She starting to get on my nerves."

"Nah, we can still use her. Wail until we empty her wallet."

"Yeah, right. You've seen how stingy she's gotten all of a sudden, after you made her put that ¥500,000 bass on her card. You spoiled it for everyone. I still had a bunch of clothes I wanted, you know."

"It wasn't ¥500,000, only ¥487,200. Anyway, it doesn't matter—it all comes out of her parents' account. They're rich country types, right? This is nothing to them, believe me. Try her and see. Take her out shopping at the end of the month. We've got two gigs coming up, right? One this month, one next month—so you've got a good excuse. She'll buy you whatever clothes you want."

"I told you, she's really started pissing me off. Just having that stupid gaping face around drives me nuts. I don't think I can take much more. And then yesterday I wrote to tell her to come over when she finished work, right, and she just totally blew me off. She's getting kind of uppity, if you ask me."

"Yeah? That does sound a bit cocky, in a subtle sort of way. You think she really believes she's our manager, that she's, like, one of us? Maybe we've been too nice."

"It's your fault—coming on to her like that. It went to her head."

"What, you think it's my fault? Shit, what a pain. She's coming tonight, right? I say we set her straight during the meeting. Tell her she's our slave, and she better act the part."

Shiori remained slumped over on the landing, unable to move. She wanted to cover her ears, but her body wouldn't move—she couldn't even raise her arms. So the conversation taking place in the lobby overhead went on pounding into her head.

Just then, someone grabbed her shoulders from behind, making her gasp. Turning back, she saw that it was Manuel.

He looked her in the eye, put a finger to his lips, then nodded twice and glanced up the stairs, his expression stern.

Fortunately, Shiori had gasped very quietly, and the two upstairs didn't appear to have heard. They went on badmouthing her as before.

Manuel indicated to Shiori with a gesture that she should stay where she was, then waited for the right moment and went upstairs himself. The mean-spirited back-and-forth gave way to a friendly exchange of pleasantries, but still Shiori remained frozen to the spot.

Maybe it would be best for her to turn on her heel and go straight home without meeting either of those two. She could write to Manuel later and have nothing more to do with the rest of the band—forget all this had ever happened. Forget it all, even school. She wouldn't have to be sad anymore, or hurt at having been taken advantage of...

Just as she was about to push past her indecision into a decision, someone else touched her shoulder, causing her to cry out once more. This time when she looked back, she found Kuniko holding her guitar case.

Before Shiori could answer Kuniko's question about what she was doing on the stairs, she heard footsteps overhead and then Tsugumi and Tetsuya yelling down into the stairwell for them to come on up. They must have heard Kuniko. They peered down from above, wide grins on their faces. Manuel stood a little distance away, his expression as serious as it had been earlier.

●

Back in her apartment, alone, Shiori sat down on her futon without turning on the lights and pulled her knees to her chest. She stayed like that for thirty or forty minutes. One by one, fleeting images of the various catastrophes that had befallen her over the past twenty-four hours—longer, actually, if she started counting from the end of the previous week—flashed through her mind. Awful as it all was, none of it inspired in her anything resembling hatred or anger. For the time being, at least, she simply didn't have the strength for such emotions. She didn't have the spirit, the passion. All she could do was keep repeating, in her heart, that she had learned nothing from the past. She had made the same mistake all over again.

Shiori had stayed with the band until they finished rehearsing, then said she couldn't join them for the meeting, and that she could no longer be their manager. She told them the truth: that her father's business had gone under, and, since she wouldn't be getting any money from home, she would have to spend even more time waiting tables. There was just no way she could keep serving as their manager, too.

The band members were cleaning up the studio as she spoke. They looked like they felt sorry for her, but no one tried to persuade her to stay on. This didn't surprise Shiori, now that she had heard Tsugumi and Tetsuya saying what they really thought of her, but it still hurt. Part of her had hoped it would turn out they hadn't really meant what they said—maybe it had all been a joke. Now that last shred of hope was gone. Tsugumi, who had tried so hard to persuade Shiori to join the band, was revealed to be a liar, a young woman with no conscience, who wanted only to take what she could. Shiori realized that now. Whenever she tried to say something, her voice shook. She was so shocked, now that she had grasped the true nature of her situation, that she couldn't even force a smile; her expression twisted itself into something else. At certain moments, as she said what she had to say, she needed to turn away to keep them from seeing her expression.

She was unsure how to broach the topic of the money they owed her. In the end, after going back and forth again and again in her mind, she decided to let everything go except for Tetsuya's bass, which she asked him to return, since she couldn't pay off the charge.

Tetsuya replied curtly that used instruments couldn't be returned, so obviously the best approach was for him to reimburse her once she had paid the credit-card company in full. Shiori, hamstrung by her ignorance of how credit cards worked, didn't know how to respond to this. She told him she wanted, at least, to try taking the bass back to the store. He refused. Plead as she might, he wouldn't listen.

In the end, Shiori thought, it's just like Nozomi said on that Christmas Eve back in high school. I can't size people up.

I'm completely incapable of seeing them as they are. Zero. I'm stupid. I'm an idiot. And so here I am, two years later, in almost exactly the same situation.

Nozomi, she cried out in her heart, begging for help telepathically.

She wanted to call home, to hear Nozomi's voice, to throw herself into her arms. But she couldn't. She had sworn not to trouble her family any further.

It was windy outside, and a light rain was falling. An approaching typhoon, maybe.

She reached out for her clock. Ten minutes earlier, the date had changed. She wanted so badly to sleep, but of course at times like these you never feel sleepy. Unable to yawn, she sighed. She didn't feel like losing herself in a TV program or on her phone. She had nothing to do, so she went on thinking, even though she had no desire to do that either.

Maybe in the morning she would go back to being her usual self. Should she try going to school? How long would it be until classes started again? Would they really share information as it came in, as they promised? What was she supposed to live for if she had to give up her studies of lyric-writing before she had accomplished anything? What reason did she have to be alive anyway?

Unaccustomed to pessimism, Shiori had no idea how to halt the downward spiral of her thoughts. It seemed they might keep going down forever. Still balled up, clutching her knees to her chest, she let herself roll sideways onto her futon. She wasn't sleepy, and she knew she would only open her eyes again if she closed them, so she let her vision rove, lingering on different areas in her apartment. It dawned on her how long it had been since she had last given it a thorough cleaning—that was how busy she had been this past month.

She was still lying there when there was a knock on the door.

Desperate though she was, she was still sane enough to know it wasn't wise to throw open her door to an unexpected visitor in the middle of the night.

The knocking continued. Though she was unnerved by the sharp, light rapping, she was also curious. Without saying anything, she walked slowly to the door and peered out through the peephole. Unfortunately, the rain had clouded the lens, and she couldn't see out.

Her heart thumping, she decided she should at least see what the person wanted. She was about to ask through the door when, amid the knocking, she heard a familiar voice.

"Shiori?"

She hadn't expected it to be anyone she knew.

"Who is it?" she asked, surprised.

"It's me," Manuel replied.

●

No sooner had Manuel stepped through the door than he began apologizing. He told her he felt absolutely terrible for having drawn her into a situation that caused her such suffering. All this had started, he said, when Tsugumi read one of their email exchanges. She had a habit of looking at other people's cell phones without their knowing. Anyone who had ever visited her apartment had gotten this treatment.

"I'm sure she checked yours, too," he said. Manuel had stayed over at Tsugumi's place a few times, and she had read his emails while he was in the shower. "She does it out of boredom," he explained, "and of course she doesn't ask."

"In your emails," Manuel continued, "you told me all about your life back home, and when Tsugumi read what you wrote she must have decided, in her sly way, that she could use you. You were an easy target, judging from what happened with your old boyfriend, Suzuki-kun. So she treated you like her own personal servant, and even took money from you. Before long Tetsuya joined in, too, following her example.

"It's all my fault, though. Obviously Tsugumi and Tetsuya are complete jerks, but I'm the one who invited you to come see us play. I'm responsible, and I feel awful about it. There's not much point in apologizing now, I guess, but even so I want you to know how sorry I am. I couldn't leave without telling you that. Please, accept my apology..."

Manuel spoke at some length, punctuating his speech with gestures. Then he handed her a hard instrument case, telling her it was hers. Inside was a brand-new electric bass—the one she had bought for Tetsuya.

Actually, Manuel said, he had just quit the band. Tetsuya hadn't willingly given the bass up, but he came around in the end.

Now that she was paying attention, it struck Shiori that Manuel's lips looked swollen.

"It's really not your fault, Manuel," Shiori said, her tone clear. "I did it to myself."

Manuel tried to protest, but she cut him off. This was her punishment for killing those parakeets.

Try as she might to persuade Manuel, he wouldn't agree. He had created the possibility. He was to blame.

"No," she said, "the blame is mine."

But he wouldn't relent.

Suddenly Shiori laughed. It had struck her how silly this was—each of them insisting on taking the blame. Manuel laughed, too.

"It's like we're in a TV drama," Shiori remarked. "People have these conversations all the time."

Manuel didn't get the allusion and stared at her blankly.

"You want some?" he asked, holding out a convenience-store bag with a sports drink inside.

Shiori went to get glasses.

"Come to think of it," Manuel said quietly, "isn't *tsugumi* a kind of bird?"

Shiori was so startled she nearly dropped the glasses. She

felt as if she had just been hit by a revelation. Her thoughts raced.

Yes, tsugumi *is a kind of bird. Tsugumi is an avatar of those birds. All of this, it's all a divine punishment. The birds have given me what I deserved.*

This was the only possible conclusion. It made perfect sense. In an instant, the fog that had clouded Shiori's mind dissipated, and a feeling of great joy welled up within her. She had succeeded in adhering to the great imperative of her life, which was atonement.

Manuel was puzzled by Shiori's reaction to his comment. He asked what had happened, and she explained as she poured the sports drink into the glasses. It had all been a test. This period in her life was all about testing her will.

Shiori continued, speaking very slowly.

It was fate, she said, that she had been treated so badly when she agreed to help out with the band. So many awful things had happened recently that it was hard to keep track of it all, it was true, but she was convinced it was all just a series of trials meant to push her, to see if she was truly committed to atoning for her sins. The trials had only just begun, and maybe it would get even worse in the future. It might. But she was still relatively well off—all around her there were people who were much, much less fortunate, much more miserable than her. She wouldn't let things get her down. She would continue to devote her life to making up for what she had done to those birds.

It wasn't clear how much of this Manuel really understood, but he was listening, regarding her attentively. He stopped trying to convince her that it was ultimately his fault. He didn't say anything; he might even have been smiling. And Shiori felt a subtle ebbing of happiness, imagining that in his heart, without speaking a word, he was agreeing with what she had said, telling her she was absolutely right.

After a while, Shiori asked Manuel something she had been wondering about. She wanted to know if he had been Tsugumi's boyfriend. Manuel admitted that they had been involved for a time and asked when she had noticed. Shiori confessed that it had only just occurred to her—his saying he had stayed at her place had put the thought in her head.

Shiori hesitated to probe any deeper into their relationship. She was feeling more and more curious by the second, but it was a private matter, and she might touch on something that would annoy him. She was so clumsy when it came to these things that she was almost certain to do exactly that. She had to restrain these base urges.

Come to think of it, she knew almost nothing about Manuel. She had been so busy since she started managing the band that she had never followed through on her plans to read up on Portugal... Realizing this reminded her of something else he had said a moment ago that had caught her notice.

She asked him about it right away. Was he going back to Portugal? He told her he was. That's why he quit the band, actually—she shouldn't blame herself. Shiori kept quiet, gazing at the floor with her head cocked.

"Please don't be sad," Manuel said, and smiled.

Shiori asked, with some hesitation, why he had to leave so suddenly. He said his job here was done. He flashed her a somewhat bashful grin.

She would have liked to ask Manuel what sort of job he had been doing, but she decided against it, afraid he might find the question prying and impolite. She herself thought she might come across as self-centered if she suddenly got all curious about his life and started peppering him with questions just because he had been nice enough to come see her, when all along she had never shown any interest in his work. Perhaps she was being paranoid, but it was better to be safe than sorry. That thoughtless message she had sent to Z, when she was giddy at having made so many new friends, had made her somewhat overcautious. She felt sure her email must have wounded him.

After debating what to say next for a while, Shiori asked when he would be leaving Japan. He gestured with his chin toward a bag he had brought. That was her answer right there, he said. In addition to the guitar case, he had with him a very large, black suitcase.

It seemed so sudden, Shiori said. He replied that he would be airborne by this time tomorrow. She asked if that was all his luggage, and he told her he had FedExed the rest. Shiori sighed, stretching out a hand to feel the surface of the suitcase.

"This thing is huge," she said, sounding a bit intimidated. "It's kind of imposing."

"Nah," Manuel responded. "You could easily carry it yourself."

●

Shiori awoke to the chirp of her alarm clock. As she rubbed the blear from her eyes, the events of the previous night gradually returned to her. But partway through her conversation with Manuel, her memories broke off. Realizing she had somehow managed to fall asleep in the middle of a conversation with her guest, she quickly looked around the room, hoping to apologize. Manuel was nowhere to be seen.

Her first guess was that he had left around the time the trains started running. That didn't seem right, though, because his giant black suitcase was still parked in the corner. He didn't appear to be in the toilet or bathroom, though, so he must have gone out.

Maybe he went on a walk, or to get breakfast? It occurred to Shiori that she could try and reach him on his phone. Standing up to get her own, she realized there was a blanket on the lower half of her body. Manuel must have put it over her when she went to sleep.

A light was flashing on her phone. She had mail. There

were three emails, in fact, all from Manuel. The subject heading of the first was "Goodbye."

Good morning! I took the liberty of leaving while you were asleep. Talking about taking liberties, I have to confess that I lied to you about something, too. I'm not actually Portuguese, and Manuel isn't my real name. I'm sorry I deceived you. I really am sorry. Fortunately, you never asked me much about my background, so I didn't have to lie too much. I was glad of that. And deeply grateful.

So who am I? Unfortunately, I can't tell you. I feel bad about that, but it wouldn't be good for either of us if I confessed things to you. Just think of me as a guy who claimed to be a Portuguese guy named Manuel. If anyone ever asks about me, just tell them I played drums in a band, and that I said my name was Manuel and that I was Portuguese. If they press you for more, show them this message.

That was the first email. The second was titled "Present."

The things I'm about to write are very, very important. I want you to note down the crucial points here, and in any other messages I may send, and then erase all my emails. It would be a pain if someone like Tsugumi were to read them without you knowing.

I'm sure you've noticed already, but I've left my suitcase in your room. I didn't forget it, don't worry—I left it on purpose. Like I wrote in the subject heading, it's a present. I'm sorry to push something so bulky off on you. But I think you'll find it useful.

The truth is, it's not an ordinary suitcase. You've probably heard the phrase "suitcase bomb" once or twice. That's what it is. But it's not an ordinary suitcase bomb. It brings together numerous refinements on earlier models. And most important, it's not a conventional bomb—it's nuclear.

What sorts of improvements have they made? I think you'll understand best if you give it a once-over yourself. It's easy—just open it up. So… what do you think? Looks like an ordinary suitcase, right? No one would ever guess that it's actually a nuclear bomb. You can take out all the clothes and everyday items I've put inside and go over it as thoroughly as you like. People would get suspicious if they ran it through a highly sensitive radiation detector, but I don't think anything in its appearance would give it away. I should note, by the way, that you don't have to worry about being exposed to radiation—it's lined with protective materials that prevent radiation from leaking out.

The bomb is known as "Mysterious Setting." Apparently, it's a term jewelers use. I don't really know the details, but from what I've been told it's a method of setting a lot of stones very close together on a base so it looks like there's nothing holding them there. The suitcase I'm giving you is kind of like that: assembled using highly advanced techniques that make it look like something it's not. There isn't a single outward sign that it's a bomb, after all. It just looks like a suitcase.

One other special thing to note is that it can go for ages without needing to have any of its parts changed. Its only drawback, if you can call it that, is that it's too big to move around easily. You can make much smaller portable nuclear bombs, but evidently it needs a certain volume to function as a "Mysterious Setting." The bulkiness is the result of certain technical requirements, in other words.

That was the second message. The subject of the third was "How to use it."

And now, how to use it. The detonator is on a timer. It has been set to give whoever activates it more than enough time to escape the range of the blast. So you don't have to worry about that. Needless to say, circumstances could still make it hard to get away, so you need to plan carefully and exercise caution in using it.

Detonating it is simple. First, take out the two keys you'll find in the inside pocket. Insert the tips of these two special keys into the holes on either side of the handle, activating the electric lock. When you do this, the three numbers in the combination below the handle will click to 000, and the timer will start. Every fifteen seconds, that number will increase by one. When it gets all the way back to 000 four hours and ten minutes later, the detonator will be activated, igniting the high-grade explosives around the baseball-sized plutonium core, causing the core to implode, reaching supercritical mass. Then comes the big boom.

If you want, you can decrease the time to detonation. All you have to do is fit those two keys into the holes and turn the numbers on the lock by hand. If you turn the lock to 500, say, then you're left with two hours and five minutes until detonation. You may find it a bit tricky to do this all yourself, but, if you experiment a bit, I'm sure you can make it work.

Finally, let me say that you are free to do as you like with the suitcase. I leave that decision to you. I was supposed to take it back to our facilities, now that I have unexpectedly been released from my duties, but, to tell the truth, I didn't expect that anything like this would happen, and I don't agree with the hasty, high-handed manner in which certain things are being pushed forward. I have no desire to accept their terms just like that. But once things have been set in motion, it's very hard to stop them. The world has begun moving toward reconciliation, whether we like it or not. Very few options have been left to me. In the end, this is what I have chosen: to put the fate of the world in your hands. I made this decision on my own, though a few members of my group who have found themselves in a similar position have told me they support what I'm doing.

I ought to have detonated the suitcase myself. Honestly, that was my plan until I went to see you last night. Talking with you changed my mind. I came to see that someone from this country ought to be allowed to decide its future. You made me see this. So I have arranged to leave Japan, together with my comrades, carrying a fake suitcase bomb. Leaving the real one with you.

The fate of the world lies with you. I don't mean to put pressure on you, of course—I don't want you to get depressed. Decide for yourself what you want to do with the bomb. That's all I hope for. I promise I won't complain, no matter how you deal with it.

I'm sure you must be feeling a bit confused, wondering why I chose you. All I can say is that you have what it takes to shoulder this responsibility. I believe that. That's why I've left it in your hands. I pray for your happiness.

●

The first thing Shiori did after she finished reading the three emails and sat for a while in stunned, breathless silence, was dial Manuel's number. He picked up immediately. When she asked where he was, he calmly gave the name of a port and said he was about to board his boat. His tone was so composed that it was hard to believe he was the same person who had just sent those messages.

Shiori had called on an impulse, and she was so bewildered that she couldn't think what she ought to ask next. Her mind was blank, and yet for some reason her lips were twitching, and her fingers were so limp she feared she might drop her phone on the floor.

"Were you surprised to see me writing so well in Japanese?" Manuel asked.

Shiori, uncertain how to respond, hummed ambiguously. She wasn't quite sure what he was asking—she wasn't together enough to listen. She heard Manuel chuckle on the other end of the line.

"You want to know if what I wrote in those emails is true, right?"

Yes, exactly. Shiori nodded rapidly and hummed again. Manuel's framing of the issue had finally brought some order to her thoughts. She had called, hoping he would tell her it was all a lie.

Manuel immediately dashed her hopes. Every word was true, he assured her, from beginning to end. She could tell from his tone that he meant it. He told her it was about time for him to go. Then, citing her own words, he shut off her final escape route.

"I'm sure you're close to panicking, having this tremendous burden thrust upon you. It's only natural to feel that way. I said you're free to do what you want with the bomb, but of course you can't be free from the enormity of the responsibility, since so many lives are at stake. You could say it's *too much* responsibility. Literally overnight, you've been invested with this extraordinary power—you'd have to be crazy not to be overwhelmed. I was assigned the same task, so I know just how you feel, I really do. And so, precisely because I sympathize so deeply, I want to say what I can to help. The thing is, I don't actually think I need to say anything, because deep in your heart, you already understand what it means, and you have for a long time. This is your fate, one of the trials you are meant to endure. You already saw your life like that, even before I gave you the suitcase. There's only one answer, now. You understand that, don't you? All right, it's time. I'm leaving Japan. If anything comes up, I'll be in touch. Goodbye."

The line went dead. He hadn't given her time to reply.

Shiori sank to the floor. The phone dropped from her limp right hand.

She was shaken. Tears streamed from her large eyes.

This whole thing felt like a story, a work of fiction. She couldn't believe it. She wept at all the terrible things that kept happening to her, one after another.

Shiori had never heard of a suitcase bomb, let alone a nuclear upgrade. This thing Manuel had brought her was so far removed from her day-to-day existence that she couldn't even begin to comprehend it. Not only had she been catapulted into a bizarre world without knowing it was happening, but it turned out even Manuel, who had been so gentle with her, so thoughtful—even he had been lying. This, too, came as a terrible shock.

The massive suitcase stood in the corner, unnervingly tall. The black matte form had an unmistakably bomb-like aura, which seemed to lend credence to everything Manuel had said in those three emails.

Suddenly, though, a doubt sprouted in her mind. He had said on the phone that it was all true, but there was no guarantee it wasn't just a cruel practical joke. She would have preferred that, actually—that the reality she was experiencing right now was rooted in a series of lies. She would much rather endure the hurt of being subjected to another heartless joke than find herself in possession of a nuclear bomb.

Much as it terrified her, she crept over to the suitcase. For the time being, at least, it was all she had to go on as she tried to decide whether or not this was real. She poked it a few times with trepidation, and then, very slowly, very carefully, she opened it.

Just as Manuel had said in his second message, the suitcase was filled with men's clothing, a shaving kit and various other ordinary items, including a weekly magazine in Japanese, a few CDs and a set of tools. There was nothing at all unusual about it. No matter what angle she examined it from, it was just a suitcase, plain and simple.

Suddenly overcome by exhaustion, Shiori stepped away from the suitcase. She picked up her cell phone and reread the second email, "Present." One passage in particular caught her eye, and she reread it several times.

Looks like an ordinary suitcase, right? No one would ever guess that it's actually a nuclear bomb. You can take out all the clothes and everyday items I've put inside and go over it as thoroughly as you like. People would get suspicious if they ran it through a highly sensitive radiation detector, but I don't think anything in its appearance would give it away.

It struck her as odd that he placed so much emphasis on how ordinary the suitcase looked. Maybe this explanation was a trap, designed to throw her off? The more she thought about it, the more her doubts turned to suspicions.

He said it was a nuclear bomb that looked exactly like a regular suitcase, but maybe this was just him trying to make a ridiculous story sound plausible. Maybe this whole thing was just a mean-spirited practical joke he was playing, using a suitcase packed with stuff he didn't need anymore, and he was off somewhere laughing at her for being so scared. For all she knew, he could be in cahoots with Tsugumi and Tetsuya, and the three of them had made her the butt of a cruel joke. In fact, she thought, that had to be it. Given the level at which Shiori generally operated, she had done a pretty good job reasoning it out, and she felt the beginnings of a newfound confidence in herself.

Maybe after being deceived by so many people she had finally matured enough to recognize the techniques people employed to trick her. That would be nice, she thought—a somewhat backwards hope. But no sooner had this occurred to her than she recalled Manuel's modesty and thoughtfulness the previous night, and she was shaken once again. If she believed he had been fooling her even during that conversation, she would basically be admitting that the world was utterly cold and unfeeling.

If society were really that twisted, how could two people ever communicate? She simply couldn't accept that everyone she ever met was constantly putting on an act—every word, every action. If that were the case, she wouldn't know what to make of anything anyone said; she would have no idea what was what. Her own words, too, would be set loose to bob through space until, like soap bubbles, they burst in the air. If words could never reach their target, then maybe there had actually never been a target.

That, Shiori realized, is why poets are so alone. In the end, all we can do is amble about, muttering to ourselves, and yet troubadours choose, even so, to sing their hearts out.

Imagining a bubble of song colliding in midair with another bubble filled with muttering, and both of them popping, Shiori felt she had understood, just a modicum better than before, the lot of the troubadour.

This was not necessarily a positive thing, however. Because it made her feel more bitter and world-weary than she ever had before. She felt as if she were gazing down at herself from someplace high above as she took her first step into a deep pool of despair.

●

Hunger finally drove Shiori to prepare a late breakfast. While she was eating, she came to the conclusion that the smart thing to do was to deliver the suitcase to the police.

It's just a suitcase. Much as Shiori tried to convince herself of this, she couldn't help handling it with extraordinary care. The remote possibility that it might actually be a nuclear weapon made her break out in a cold sweat as she dragged it down the street, over the asphalt. Each time a car whizzed past she gave a start and came very close to hyperventilating.

No one was at the nearest police box when she arrived— the officer on duty must have been out making the rounds. The whole trip had been a waste. It had been so harrowing to get here, though, that she didn't want to go back to her apartment and come again later. After steadying the suitcase in what seemed like a safe spot just off the sidewalk, she squatted down outside the police box to wait.

Tokyo had been windy the previous evening, and there had even been some rain, but this morning there wasn't a cloud in the sky. Sitting in the hot sun made Shiori's head ache, and soon she was feeling ill. Her breathing grew heavier, and she couldn't stop yawning. She needed something to drink, but she lacked the energy to drag the suitcase to a vending machine or convenience store. Uh-oh, she thought weakly—I'm going to throw up. Just then a uniformed police officer rode up on a bicycle.

The middle-aged man offered her a cup of cold barley tea even before he asked why she was there. He seemed to think she might be succumbing to heat stroke. Shiori was pleased: he was a good man, she could tell—someone she could trust. And so she launched into her story about the suitcase. The result, however, was not what she had expected. The first thing he said when she finished talking was that since it wasn't a lost item, the police couldn't take it off her hands. Shiori was so taken aback that for a moment she just gaped. Then she told him again that it wasn't hers. The officer simply shook his head. Unable to see any other way forward, Shiori showed him the three emails from Manuel, but even then all she managed to get out of him was a repetition of the point that rules were rules.

"See here, he says he's giving it to you as a present, right? So it's yours, no doubt about it. You can't bring presents to the police just because you don't like them. Our storage facilities would fill up in no time if we had to take everyone's unwanted gifts. We're the police, you know—we don't do waste disposal. If you don't need the suitcase, arrange to have it picked up by the sanitation department or sell it to a second-hand shop or something. How's that sound?"

Was he intentionally ignoring the most crucial part? Her face flushed, Shiori tried pointing out, sharply for her, that the suitcase could well contain a nuclear bomb.

"Hee-hee. Listen, I don't want to be rude, but I get the sense you're kind of gullible, huh? Am I correct? Yes, you are. So let me tell you what you should do here, OK? You're still in touch with this guy? Well then, just wait for him to contact you. And then you say to him, straight out, 'Look, I don't need your dumb suitcase, OK, so come back and get it.' You have to solve this one on your own, in other words. You understand? Ah, one other thing, just in case. This guy hasn't, like, tricked you out of a lot of money or anything, has he? No? Well, that's all right then. Glad everything has worked out."

He was a nice man, but disappointingly inflexible. At the same time, Shiori herself had no proof that the suitcase really was a bomb, so she had no grounds for pushing harder. She thanked the officer for the tea and walked out of the police box.

It took Shiori longer to get back to her apartment, pulling the suitcase behind her, than it had to get to the police box. She was so disappointed she couldn't help dragging her feet, but the heat was also getting to her.

Back in her apartment, she turned on the air conditioner, pushed the suitcase back into its corner, then went straight to the refrigerator. There was some of the sports drink Manuel had brought left. She flopped down on the floor with the bottle and set about finishing it. After that, she felt too weary to stand up, so she crawled like a baby over to her futon, which she hadn't yet folded up and put away.

Lying on her back, she began to regret not going to school. She put her arms up by her head. She tried to check the clock, but it was hard to make out from the position she was in, and she gave up after a few seconds.

Though she couldn't get a good look at the face of the clock, which was right next to her, the suitcase way over in the corner was almost oppressively *there*.

It had never occurred to Shiori that the police might refuse to take the suitcase from her, and she could think of no other way to rid herself of it. She was completely at a loss. She could have put an ordinary suitcase out with the oversized trash or sold it to a second-hand shop, but she couldn't ignore the possibility that it might be a bomb, so neither route was available to her now. Pushing the suitcase off on someone who didn't know what it was would mean repeating Manuel's irresponsibility.

Eventually, in the course of her thinking, Shiori fell asleep. And as she slept, her breathing deep and slow, she dreamed. She saw herself taking the suitcase out of her apartment in the dead of night, hiding it in the bushes in a large park nearby.

Soon day broke, and, as the sun climbed higher, people began gathering in the park—an old man doing morning exercises, an old woman walking a dog, children frolicking on the swings and the jungle gym. Shiori was watching over these people when she realized that she was no longer a person: somehow her body had been transformed into a little bird, and she was flitting about freely in the sky, able to take in the entire park.

The little bird Shiori felt marvelous, dancing through the sky on her wings. She spun and spun, whirled and twirled, on and on, high above the park. She could soar so easily through the air, fly effortlessly in any direction she pleased—though gradually she began to realize that the range of her flight was limited to the space within the contours of the park.

That evening, the bird Shiori fluttered down onto the suitcase to rest her wings. She was straightening her feathers with her beak when a second- or third-grade boy appeared, pushing through the foliage, causing her instinctively to dart up into the air and take refuge within the shadowy foliage of a tree. She remained there only a moment, though, before she swooped back down onto the suitcase. It had occurred to her the boy might take the suitcase home.

He showed no interest in doing that. Instead, he set about activating the timer on the bomb, using two keys he had taken from the suitcase. Shiori noticed that he had her cell phone and was consulting Manuel's directions as he worked.

The bird Shiori perched on the suitcase's handle and chirped with all her might, trying to persuade the boy to stop, but he batted her away violently. Thrown against the trunk of a tree, then further wounded by the fall, she lay motionless on the ground. She knew she had to stop the boy, whatever it took, even if it meant dashing herself against his hands, and she struggled desperately to fly again... But the bones in her wings and feet were broken. She couldn't do a thing.

The boy was spinning the numbers on the lock, more and more—he must have shrunk the time until the bomb detonated considerably. Indeed, he seemed to have rotated the dials more than he meant to, because all of a sudden he let go of the suitcase and sprinted away as fast as his legs would carry him.

The next instant, the suitcase exploded. The blast flung the bird Shiori high into the sky, where she was sucked inside the billowing mushroom cloud. Engulfed in scorching heat, she nonetheless remained whole, burned but not consumed, trapped in a world that was no longer anything at all but a gray, soundless vacuum.

Waking from her doze, Shiori quickly reached for the clock. It was 2:45 p.m. She leapt up, relieved that she could still make it to work on time. Her boss would be furious if she were late again, after oversleeping yesterday. She had gotten up from her futon so quickly that her head spun, but she didn't even wait for the dizziness to subside before going into the modular bathroom and washing her face.

●

On Wednesday, she went to school. There was no crowd of students outside the building, as there had been on Monday and the previous Friday, but school remained closed. A notice on the front door, evidently posted the day before, explained that since it was still unclear when classes would be able to start again, the administration had decided to begin summer vacation early. Students would be contacted as soon as the dates for the new semester had been fixed. Shiori thought it odd that they hadn't reached out to students directly about this summer vacation plan earlier if that was the direction they were heading in.

She had a lot to think about on the subway back to her apartment.

What would she do if the school closed for good? She had paid them more than eight hundred thousand yen to cover enrollment, the year's tuition, teaching materials, facility fees and whatever else they charged her for. She had attended only two months of classes, from April to June, so they ought at least to refund the rest. If she could get that money back, maybe it would make life a little easier for her parents and Nozomi—and, of course, the cats. There must be some way to follow up on that.

Back in her apartment, Shiori wondered how she should use all the extra time she had now. She had signed up to work at the restaurant from 4:00 p.m. today, and tomorrow, and the next day. Over the coming days, then, she would be at a loose end until late afternoon. Maybe she should look for another job? She would have to earn a lot more to cover her rent and living expenses...

Then, out of the blue, she felt a different pressure.

Hey. Hey! Don't you ignore me. You see me over here, right? Quit acting like you don't. You can't fool me. Trying to act like you you're not interested when really you can't put me out of your thoughts—I see it all. Your finances aren't exactly the most pressing of your worries, are they? Don't turn your back on the real problem. Don't you think, Shiori darling, that it's time you accept the situation and start thinking seriously about how you're going to dispose of me? Hey. Hey! What are you going to do? Hurry up and decide, will you? Nothing good will come from leaving me here like this, you know.

Shiori protested that she wasn't ignoring the suitcase, but the suitcase kept glaring at her with the same menacing air. She was so scared that she sat up properly with her legs tucked under her and bowed an apology in its direction.

Shiori darling, I don't need your apologies. Just start thinking.

The suitcase kept pressing her to find a solution, but she didn't see how she could. She had been considering her options ever since it arrived in her apartment the day before, even without it hounding her like this—the problem was that none of the options was any good. That's exactly why she was trying to lose herself in everyday things.

She hated having it in her apartment, and yet she couldn't just throw it out. If only she could find some way to demonstrate conclusively that it was a genuine nuclear bomb, then the police would have no option but to take it off her hands. She had no idea what sort of evidence she needed, though. She would have liked to ask a professional to inspect it, but since the police officer had laughed in her face and even Z had stopped answering the emails she sent asking for advice, she assumed she would be chased off the grounds of whatever institution or organization she tried to visit before she could get a foot in the door.

Yes, that's right. The previous night, Shiori had told Z everything that had happened. By now, he was the only one she could turn to—and he hadn't replied.

Hoping to persuade him that the issue she needed help with was real, unrealistic though it might sound, she had explained everything in as much detail as possible in several separate emails. She had started the first email at work, during break, and finished the last in the early hours of the morning.

Already more than twelve hours had passed since she sent that series of emails to Z. He had never been so slow to reply in the past. Maybe even he had been taken aback, uncertain how to respond to her plea for help. This tribulation had been visited upon her; in the end, it seemed, it would to be up to her to find a solution.

Come to think of it, she mused, her relationship with Manuel's band had followed precisely the trajectory Z had warned her it would. Maybe, if she had listened to him, she wouldn't have had to shoulder this new burden. To make matters worse, she had concluded that the advice he gave her, purely out of the goodness of his heart, was a sign he envied her good fortune, because his own condition prevented him from going out and meeting friends. She had, she saw, been doubly rude and insensitive.

She would have liked to apologize right away, but she decided against it, fearing this would only annoy him. From his perspective, it must have been pretty galling for her to come crying to him about a situation that only arose because she ignored his advice. She couldn't think of anything more self-centered, in fact, than to act as she had done, contacting him without a second thought as soon as she realized this suitcase was more than she could handle alone.

Shiori regretted from the bottom of her heart that she had turned to Z for help. And she was utterly disgusted with herself. Why hadn't she thought about these things beforehand? She pressed her face so forcefully into her pillow that it felt like her nose would break. She tried to wail, too, but by then her body would no longer permit either cries or tears.

●

Hey. Hey! Shiori, darling. What's up, Suity? **Where are you taking me today?** Hmm. Where should we go? **Someplace with a view would be nice. That's what I'd like.** Why? **Better to be somewhere where you don't get bored, don't you think? Where you've got the scenery to look at.** I see your point. Yeah. **Besides, that'll be better for you, too, right?** Why's that? **If you change your mind about one spot, having seen it, it's easy to search out a new target if you've got a nice, long view.** A target? What do you mean? **A target's a target.** I don't get what you're talking about. **Don't play dumb. I know you're thinking of testing me, my powers.** Your powers? **I said not to play dumb. You know very well what I am.** No, I don't. **Listen, let's put an end to this game of yours. I'll tell you myself: I'm a nuclear bomb. With a timed detonator, I might add.** I have no evidence of that. **You will if you detonate me.** No. **It's the easiest way to check.** No way. **The thing is, that's what you're thinking.** No, it isn't. I'm definitely not thinking of that. **You're not going to confess?** But I really don't! **Admit it.** You're annoying. **Whatever. Eventually, you'll have to.** No, I won't. **Yes, you will.** I definitely will *not*. **Oh yes, you will!** Oh no, I won't! **You're one stubborn girl.** Right back at you, Suity. **I wouldn't say that about me.** Wouldn't you? **No, I wouldn't.** See! **What do you mean *see!*** A typical obstinate middle-aged man. **Excuse me?** See, you're mad. **Shut up.** You're annoyed because I'm right. **Little shit.** Just listen to you, cursing like that. If you keep talking back, I won't take you anywhere. You understand, Suity?

Ten days had passed since Shiori found herself living with the suitcase, and at some point she had begun calling it "Suity." At first, she had been so scared that she always talked very politely with it, but when it kept trying to strike up conversations, again and again, to the point that it started getting irritating, she began talking back. By now she felt comfortable enough with it—with him—that they could joke around, tossing sarcastic remarks back and forth. That they had grown so close so quickly was a sign, of course, of how dependent they were on each other. Shiori had no one but Suity to talk to; and from Suity's perspective, Shiori was a thoughtful owner who took him on regular walks, leading him by the handle to all kinds of interesting places.

These aimless outings had been part of their daily routine for the past several days. On weekdays she took him out before work; on weekends, they visited different areas of the city that they could reach by train during the few hours left after she got off from work.

Before they started making these trips, Shiori had found it difficult to bear Suity's persistent questions. **So, what are you going to do with me?** he kept asking, trying to force her to make a decision. He came at her constantly, even when she was asleep, until it became unendurable. She had to find a way to escape that voice.

At first, she had wandered out, hoping to find some shadowy, hidden place where she could leave the suitcase without worrying that anyone might find it, but this hadn't worked out. When she imagined the consequences if the bomb were somehow detonated where she left it—deep in the thickets of a public park, on the banks of one of Tokyo's rivers, at the foot of a mountain outside the city, behind a pile of refuse somewhere in town, in an abandoned building, in an alleyway...—her determination faltered.

Whatever place she chose, the plants and animals and people who lived around it would have no way of escaping the destruction wrought by the blast. The more she rode around on different trains, searching for a suitable location for the suitcase's disposal, the more deeply it was borne upon her that there was simply nowhere in the world where you could leave a nuclear bomb. In the end, she always brought it back to her apartment.

She finally gave up on the idea of abandoning the suitcase, though through force of habit she continued to take it out. Lugging the suitcase here and there for no reason had come, you see, to provide her with just a modicum of comfort.

For the past month, Shiori had been so absorbed in her classes at school, and in her work, and in doing odd jobs for the band, that the scenery gliding past the windows of the trains as they rushed through the city struck her with a wonderful freshness and lightened her mood, if only a little. She felt like a tourist out seeing the sights of Tokyo with Suity, and that helped liberate her from reality, if only for a time, and curb her reclusive impulses.

Since she was devoting so much time to these little trips, she had to put off returning the electric bass Manuel had given her. She had to find another job to help pay the rent and cover her living expenses, she knew that, but she wanted to spend at least a little more time living like this, seeing the world like a traveler.

Her life with Suity wasn't so bad. Early on, she had found his constant talking irritating, but now that she was used to it, she didn't mind. Actually, she kind of liked it that he rattled on like that—she felt very alone in Tokyo, now that she no longer had any contact with her family and had lost her only friends in the city.

That time when she had gone to the police box, hoping the officer might take the suitcase off her hands, she had been absurdly nervous just dragging it a few meters over the pavement; now she wasn't so cautious. Gradually, their daily promenades were teaching her to steer the suitcase more nimbly, with one hand on the handle. She didn't cut a figure quite as dashing as a pilot or flight attendant, but she could slide the suitcase rapidly along without bumping up against signs or people's legs. Like a seasoned traveler, she felt fine making her way along even the busiest streets.

Shiori liked the name Suity. She was starting to feel a certain affection for Suity himself, too. He could be cutting when he wanted to, but somehow she couldn't dislike him. Sure, he was huge, solidly built, and a dark shade of black, but there was something adorable about him, too, when you realized how needy he was—that he couldn't even leave the house without having someone else take him.

Suity was focused on only one thing: detonation. Shiori frequently found herself having to placate him on this front. He would try one approach after the next, doing his best to cajole her into setting him off. He tried asking her to talk the issues through with him, hoping he could plant the same desire in her heart. Shiori never fell for it, though, and usually managed to brush him off fairly lightly. In some ways, it was troublesome having to deal with him when he was in these moods, but it was also kind of fun—as if they were a pair of comics doing a stand-up routine.

Today, Shiori decided to let Suity have what he wanted: she would take him someplace with a view. Imagining the ocean breeze playing on her skin persuaded her to choose Odaiba. They took the subway to Shinbashi, then transferred to the Yurikamome Line and rode to Odaiba Seaside Park. All in all, it took just under an hour. Shiori had never been on the Yurikamome Line before, so she boarded the first car and stood pressed against the window, staring out at the scenery while the train rocked her back and forth. When the train headed out onto Rainbow Bridge shortly after pulling away from Shibaura-futō, she was so moved she couldn't help crying out in delight like a child.

Even before lunch, Seaside Park was as crowded as it always is in summer. Shiori ambled along the boardwalk toward the beach. The sight of children frolicking along the water's edge and shirtless youths tanning themselves on the sand made her feel all warm and toasty inside. The thumping of the suitcase's wheels as they rolled across the boardwalk was surprisingly loud. She grinned sheepishly, embarrassed by the noise, even as, on some level, she enjoyed it. Those were Suity's footsteps, after all.

She debated going down onto the beach but jettisoned that idea when she realized the suitcase would get covered in sand. She would go explore another place instead. After getting a Big Mac and a ginger ale for lunch at the McDonald's on the first floor of DECKS Tokyo Beach Seaside Mall, she went up to the observation deck in the skywalk, where they could see the replica of the Statue of Liberty up close. She steadied the suitcase so it wouldn't fall, then sat down on a bench to eat.

Well? How's this, Suity? Are you satisfied? **Hmm. It's not bad.** The view is beautiful, huh? You can see the ocean, Rainbow Bridge, the high-rises, all at once. **That's true. Yeah, I can't complain.** You can't complain, but it could be better? **That's not what I'm saying.** It's OK, I'm open to requests if you'd rather go somewhere else, as long as it's not too far. **No, this is fine.** Really? It's not like you to be so accommodating. **Actually, Shiori darling, when you finish your lunch, I was thinking... Why don't we just go ahead and do it, OK?** Do what? **C'mon, you know! Activate my timer.** Give me a break. You know I'm not going to do that. **You just said you were taking requests.** I am, if there's somewhere in particular you want to go. **Well, what I'd like is to explode, OK? To make**

the leap into an entirely different world… Sorry, too far. Not going there.

As she polished off her Big Mac, Shiori gazed out past Rainbow Bridge at the buildings of the Minato and Chūō Districts. Among the high rises was a tall, pointed brownish-red tower. It was hard to make out from here, but she figured it must be Tokyo Tower.

Hey, Suity. How about going to Tokyo Tower next? **What's that?** Tokyo Tower. See, that's it over there—like a little toy made out of wire. **Oh, I see. Yeah, that looks kind of nice.** Tomorrow's Saturday, so we'll have to wait until I finish work, but that's OK, right? **Anytime is fine with me, kid. Morning, night—all the same to me.**

●

When they got back from Odaiba, Shiori put the suitcase back in its accustomed position, took a shower and changed into some new clothes, and then headed off to work. She used her break to check the hours for Tokyo Tower on her phone.

The observation decks opened at 10:00 a.m., and the final admission was at 9:45 p.m. for the main observatory, 150 meters above ground, and 9:30 p.m. for the so-called special observatory, which was another 100 meters up. Even if they went after work the next day, they would have time to look around. Shelling out the cost of the ticket would be painful now that she had to pay her own expenses, but, since she planned to start a second job the following week, she felt justified allowing herself one last luxury.

After getting off work at 10:00 p.m., she walked along a shopping arcade near her apartment and passed a few young couples holding guitar cases outside the studio where, until recently, she had spent so much time. The sight gave her a start, but she needn't have worried—there was no one she knew.

She hadn't seen Tsugumi, Tetsuya or Kuniko once since they last parted, and she had no way of knowing whether they were even playing together as a band anymore, now that Manuel had left Japan. They had never paid her back, but until she saw those other couples on the street, she had forgotten about that, too—just as perfectly as she had forgotten them. That's how big the shock Manuel gave her had been. Of course, that didn't mean she wanted to see any of them, and it seemed unlikely to her that she ever would.

This assumption was proven wrong almost immediately. Because all of a sudden, Shiori remembered something that made her eager to talk to Tsugumi: the fact that she and Manuel had once been romantically involved. Perhaps Tsugumi had heard something from him about his background, who he was. If so, that information might help her either confirm the things he had written in his emails and told her over the phone, or else give credence to the possibility that he had been pulling her leg.

If Manuel had been lying about anything, then it seemed more likely that the suitcase was not, in fact, a bomb. This was how Shiori saw things.

And so, rather than go home, she started running toward Sangenjaya Station.

She boarded an outbound train and got off at Komazawa-daigaku, one stop away. No sooner was she through the ticket gate than she started running again. Soon she was standing outside Tsugumi's one-room apartment, Room 202—located, as the listing had said, a mere ten-minute walk from the station. The same apartment she been summoned to any number of times during the month of June.

The sprint there and the nervous excitement of being outside that door again had driven the exhaustion of work from her body, and she banged quite vigorously on the door, despite the late hour. After fourteen or fifteen tries, it finally occurred to her that Tsugumi might not be home. Thrusting her hand into the tote bag she had slung over her shoulder, she groped around until she found her phone, then flipped it open. She was still peering at her address book when Tsugumi opened the door and leaned out with a toothbrush in her mouth.

Tsugumi's eyes met Shiori's. She mumbled a few garbled, toothbrushy words.

Shiori shook her head to show she hadn't understood.

Tsugumi detached the toothbrush from her mouth and said bluntly, "If it's money you want, I don't have any."

"Huh?" Shiori replied, not quite intentionally. Then, shaking her head again, she explained that that wasn't why she had come.

Tsugumi remained brusque after she invited Shiori inside, making no effort to conceal her displeasure at having to do so. The room was as messy as ever, things scattered all across the floor. Tsugumi disappeared for a moment into the modular bathroom, then called out, between gargles, that a friend was coming to pick her up in his car at 1:00 a.m. Shiori promised she would be done within an hour. The hands on the clock pointed to 10:39 p.m. During the time it took Tsugumi to finish with her teeth and then come out, cosmetics in hand, and get settled on the edge of her bed, Shiori found herself disposing of the little bits of trash on the table, just as she had the previous month. She couldn't help herself.

At last, Tsugumi asked irritably what Shiori wanted, and Shiori explained, without beating about the bush, that she needed to know about Manuel. Tsugumi asked in a sort of eye-rolling tone of voice why Shiori thought she would know any more than she herself did, to which Shiori responded that Manuel said they had been dating. She didn't let up when Tsugumi huffed that that meant nothing—please, she pleaded, please. Tsugumi said she'd share what she knew, on one condition. What was that? Shiori would have to forget the money Tsugumi owed her. Shiori nodded, relieved, and said that was fine. She really needed to know who Manuel was.

According to Tsugumi, Manuel was a liar. He was a real swindler, the genuine article. At one point or another, he had taken in everyone in the band.

"I met him at this club, you know, and from that first night it was just this constant barrage of random stuff—I don't think he ever once said anything a person could take seriously. And he'd be so earnest about it, you know? That's what made it really bad. Then you'd go to him later to complain, when you realized he'd been messing with you, right, and he was absolutely fine just blowing you off, saying he didn't know what you were talking about. At first it was kind of fun, you know, and I thought he was cool, and of course he was really one for drama, so I had him join the band. But after maybe three months of going out with him I got fed up and broke it off. We were both still in the band, of course, so for a while it was kind of hard to make things final—we'd get together again, then break up again. He'd come stay here pretty often, claiming he'd just happened to miss the last train. Yeah, he was a talker. It seemed like he was always changing jobs, and he had a different story every time you talked to him, so I can't really tell you anything accurate. I just don't know. The only thing I can say for sure is that that guy was one big liar."

Shiori decided to take the rather bold step of sharing the emails Manuel had sent her just before he left Japan.

"Excuse me? Why the hell would I go through his emails when he wasn't looking? Now that really pisses me off. Can you believe it? He told you that, seriously? Yeah, OK, so that's another of his lies. Anyway, this sort of ludicrous, full-of-himself mouthing off is exactly the kind of thing he couldn't help doing, OK? He was taking you for a ride, obviously, no question. He pulled the same sort of thing on us, too, soon after we got to know him. Really, I'm telling you, that's his thing. I can tell you with absolute confidence that this email is total bullshit. I mean, even this name he gives it, Mysterious Setting... *I'm* the one who told him about that. You want to see the proof?"

Tsugumi bent down and pulled a stack of fashion magazines out from under her bed, then opened one and held it out. It was a spread of photos in a special feature on jewelry. Before long, Shiori spotted those words, "Mysterious Setting," in one of the captions.

●

Shiori ran on the way back, too. This time it was mostly because she was afraid she might miss the last train, but she was also feeling overjoyed and buoyant.

Back in Sangenjaya, she was so happy she decided to drop by the convenience store and buy a few things. She got bread for her warm sandwiches, a pack of KitKats, a box of mochi ice cream, a carton of coffee-flavored milk, a set of animal-character stickers and a white permanent marker. A sudden desire to celebrate had pushed her toward sweets.

She couldn't have been more pleased that Suity was just a suitcase.

First, she gave Suity a face, drawing small eyes and a nose and mouth on the body of the suitcase with the white marker. She drew flowers on the handle and in a few other spots. Then came the animal stickers, which she stuck on, more or less at random. In no time at all, his somewhat menacing demeanor had been softened and fancified.

Suity seemed not to like having these things done to him, because he refused to respond to anything Shiori said. Even when she apologized and offered to remove the stickers, he kept silent. She had to give up on celebrating with him. After assuring him that she was still going to take him to Tokyo Tower the following day, she sat down and ate her sweets by herself, feeling very alone.

Before she went to bed, she deleted the three emails from Manuel. She felt a deep sense of relief as she expunged the data— "How to use it," "Present," "Goodbye," in that order—knowing she would no longer be led astray by their lies.

After that, she wrote to Z again. He had never responded to her earlier emails, but it still seemed wrong to leave him hanging when she had worried him with all her pleading for advice. She put together a diary-like email looking back over the past ten days, going through all that had happened. She was typing while lying down, however, and midway through composing the email her eyelids began to droop, and she fell asleep before she could finish it.

●

Shiori was awake before her alarm could rouse her. Looking at her right hand, she realized she was still clutching her cell phone.

She sat up, yawned and began reading over the email she had started. Waking up to the knowledge that Suity wasn't a bomb, she found herself enveloped in a sense of joy and relief that felt different, deeper, than her emotions the previous night. Eager to communicate the sequence of events that led to this feeling, she got back to work on her email to Z.

She showered, then ate breakfast while staring distractedly at the TV. Her meal was the same as always: a warm sandwich, tomato juice, a lactoferrin-rich yogurt.

There was a news program on. She flicked through a bunch of channels, but that was all there was, just a bunch of morning news programs, so she went back to the first channel and put down the remote. The anchors were just switching from the national to the international news. The woman anchor, suddenly assuming a grave expression, explained that she would now give a recap of the morning's lead story. There had been a large explosion in the city of Sonmiani, Pakistan, not far from the country's largest city, Karachi. Sonmiani was home to a missile test facility, and while the details remained unclear it was thought the explosion may have been the result of an accident during a test. The word *explosion* made Shiori's shoulders tense for a moment, but she relaxed when she saw the suitcase, now covered in stickers.

Her phone's battery had gone dead, so she put the charger in her tote bag and set out for work. She would plug it in there.

When the time came for her break, she went and got her recharged phone and found an email waiting. It was from Z; the subject heading was "That's a relief." It seemed his failure to respond hadn't been a sign that he was sick of her, after all. He had been taken aback, uncertain how to respond, but he had gone on thinking even so about how she ought to deal with the situation. He had been trying to come up with something to tell her, researching suitcase nukes online, watching movies about terrorists. Shiori was deeply touched.

The reason he hadn't been able to write back all this time, even after doing this research, was that he had been in the hospital to take some tests. "The results were good, so that's a relief, too," he had written. Those words brought tears to her eyes.

She sent him a reply titled "Happy to hear that."

And he shot back: "Thanks!"

She was supposed to get off work at 5:00 p.m., but she ended up having to stay until 7:30 because the college student who was going to take her place came late. She bought two *onigiri* and a bottle of tea at the convenience store, which she scarfed down at her apartment before setting out with Suity to see the sights of Tokyo together one last time.

●

Having changed to the Toei Ōedo Line at Aoyama-itchōme, they pulled into Akabanebashi Station at 8:41 p.m. Stepping out onto the street at the top of the escalator, Shiori saw a brightly illuminated Tokyo Tower rising into the darkness before her, looking a bit faded and blurred in the mist.

She bought a ticket in Foot Town, on the first floor, then took the direct elevator up to the main observatory. The first thing she wanted to do was go up to the second level and look through the pay-to-use binoculars, but when she went upstairs she discovered that it was so full of couples that there was no room for her and her own date, the suitcase. She would have liked to chat with Suity as they sat gazing out over the nightscape, but she felt awkward amid the crush of lovers, and in any event she had to wander around, looking for a place to sit. After five or six minutes' circling like a roulette wheel, the suitcase's wheels squeaking behind her, she stopped by the booth selling tickets to the special observatory.

She might as well. After all, this was Suity's last look at Tokyo.

That was what she tried to tell herself, anyway. Really, she was just trying to escape the wrenching loneliness she felt. In the main observatory she found herself eyeing the couples around her rather than the scenery beyond the windows, and was overwhelmed by a feeling of utter loneliness that until then she had managed to suppress. Suity, meanwhile, was keeping quiet, perhaps out of deference to her discomfort. Paying six hundred yen for a ticket to the special observatory was really just a passive attempt to get away.

In the elevator, she discovered she wasn't the only person there alone. He stepped in after her, and after a few more couples. She had trouble making out his face or even getting a sense of his age because he had a baseball cap pulled down low over his eyes and a beard covered most of the rest. Feeling somehow disappointed, she hung her head with a sigh.

The special observatory wasn't as bad as the main observatory, but there were still a lot of couples. Now that she thought about it, not many people would pick a date as the best time to skimp on six hundred yen. Still, she tried to put the happy couples out of her mind and started making the rounds, looking for an open space with a good view.

The circle of blue lights shining out across the floor in the dimly lit observatory went on and on, giving the space a sort of sci-fi vibe. Here she was in what might have been a spaceship, wandering aimlessly around with a suitcase in tow. Outside, the nightscape of the city center opened before her in a gorgeous panorama, like a mass of bioluminescent deep-sea creatures, glowing as they dangled motionless in the water. She couldn't make up her mind where to stop. And then, after she had been walking for some time, it dawned on her that the creepy-looking guy from the elevator was following her. He kept his distance, but he had been walking in the same direction as her the entire time, and every so often their eyes would meet—this was what told her she was right. She would have liked to immerse herself in the scenery, but he kept distracting her, tagging along behind her in this weird way so that she didn't feel like she could stop, until finally she felt so unnerved that she fled into the bathroom.

The stall was too narrow for her to bring the suitcase in with her, so she had to park it outside while she took care of her business. As she sat on the toilet, she heard someone walk in and do something that produced a sort of metallic clicking noise, then walk right back out again. Shiori had a bad feeling about this, so she yanked up her underwear, flushed the toilet, and hurriedly opened the door. Just as she expected, the suitcase was gone. Someone had made off with Suity. She ran out without even washing her hands.

Half panicking, Shiori made a quick dash around the special observatory. She didn't see anyone with a suitcase. What should I do? she asked herself again and again, repeating the phrase so often she started to feel as if she were losing her hearing. She should never have hidden in the toilet, of all places—she cursed herself for doing that. It felt like having her guts ripped out of her body, being unexpectedly separated from Suity like this. And she was scared, so scared she couldn't take it. Her head filled with fog, and then she was tripping over herself, losing all sense of anything but the beating of her own heart.

Suddenly, someone tapped her on the shoulder from behind. She turned to see a man and a woman, college students by the look of them, glaring at her.

"Your suitcase, right?" said the man.

"Yes!" she cried.

"Some creep just got into the elevator with it."

Shiori thanked the couple, bowed deeply and sprinted off toward the elevator.

The man and woman were nice enough, and concerned enough, to follow. They tried to encourage her, assuring her he had only just left so she was sure to catch him, she would get her suitcase back.

When the elevator door opened at the main observatory, the couple ran out even faster than Shiori could, heading for the down elevator. Bounding along a few meters behind them, she heard cries of "Thief! Thief!" There was a cluster of people up ahead, and, as she drew near, she realized that the bearded man was in the middle, pinned to the floor by a few other men. He had just been walking into the elevator when the couple started yelling, and the rest of the people nearby had all sprung to action, joining forces to catch the thief. Shiori was moved to tears by this vision of good will, and her voice, ragged by now, quivered as she went around thanking everyone.

Two security guards had immediately run over when they heard the uproar. The couple explained what had occurred, and the suitcase was returned to Shiori. The guards seemed to have figured out on their own that it was hers, tipped off by the flowery handle and the animal stickers. Shiori, meanwhile, realizing for the first time just how much affection she had developed for Suity, knelt down and gave him a hug.

As the suitcase was being handed back over to Shiori, the bearded man began struggling violently, firing out a rapid stream of incomprehensible words, so that the two guards and a few other men had to wrestle him down again. Shiori, too frightened to look, pressed her forehead against the suitcase. One of the guards advised her to go back down to ground level, and the couple led her into the elevator. Shiori was still so shaken by the sudden turn of events that she couldn't say a word all the way down.

Back outside, she finally succeeded in calming herself. She bowed again and again to the couple, telling them she couldn't thank them enough for all they had done. They told her they had seen the guy emerge from the women's bathroom with the suitcase and figured he must have stolen it. They even offered to drive her home, since they had come by car, but Shiori didn't want to trouble them any more than she already had. As they headed off toward the parking lot, she bowed deeply several times more.

As she walked slowly down the road back to Akabanebashi Station, her cell phone chimed, alerting her to the arrival of a new email. It was from Z, and the subject was "How was Tokyo Tower?" "I hear they're going to stop using Tokyo Tower as a radio tower, since they're getting ready to start construction on a new tower by the end of the year," he had written, among other things. Once she was on her subway, Shiori slumped back in her seat and wrote a reply. She included a description of everything that had just happened.

●

Shiori got back to her apartment at around 10:10 p.m. After wheeling the suitcase into its spot, she stripped off her clothes and went to have a bath. All that running around had left her very sweaty.

When she finished toweling herself and blow-drying her hair, she threw on a T-shirt and underwear and collapsed on her futon. She was exhausted after working since morning and then having all that excitement at Tokyo Tower in the evening, and she needed to be at work again the next morning. Going to sleep right away seemed like a good idea.

She was drifting off with the lights still on when she heard a voice.

Shiori darling, Shiori darling... it came intermittently, sounding a bit crusty and peevish, and yet, at the same time, impossible to dislike—perhaps, depending on how you looked at it, even somewhat likable.

Shiori groaned, covering her eyelids with her hands.

Shiori darling, Shiori darling, Shiori darling...

Suity? Nozomi? Still covering her eyes with her hands, she called back to the voice. There was no answer to her question, though, only the same repetition of her name: Shiori darling, Shiori darling. *Ah, I see,* Shiori thought. *It's all in my head, I'm hallucinating.* Only then did she realize that it was actually her phone ringing, and she sat up.

The phone had stopped ringing by the time she got it, and when she checked the call log all it said was "Unknown number." She was still eyeing the screen suspiciously, assuming it had been either a wrong number or some sort of scam, when the phone rang again. This time she answered. The voice that came over the line belonged to the man who had thrust her into the restless world she had been inhabiting.

"Shiori? It's me, Manuel."

Shiori's breath caught in her throat. She said nothing. Not because she didn't want to, but because she couldn't. Manuel sounded so agitated, as if he had run through all his options and was now absolutely at his wit's end, that she felt herself on the verge of being drawn in once again by a lie. Terrified that a few words from Manuel were about to throw all the things that had just settled neatly into place back into disarray, she hesitated, wondering if she ought to hang up before he could say any more.

"You don't have to talk if you don't want to. I don't have much time, so I'll keep it short. Things are bad. You may have seen reports about the explosion in Sonmiani yesterday. What I'm hearing is that it was the same sort of device I gave you—there was a malfunction. They don't know what exactly went wrong, but at present the best explanation is intensive exposure to electromagnetic radiation. I'll call you again as soon as they get a definitive answer, but for the time being, keep the suitcase away from that sort of radiation, OK? Please. Otherwise, I'm worried the same thing will happen to yours..."

Before Manuel could continue, Shiori broke her silence. There was one thing she wanted to say. Tensing her stomach, summoning every last ounce of strength in her body, she asked him if he could swear that what he was saying was true.

"Yes, I can. There's no doubt about this—you've got a serious crisis heading toward you right now. Actually, things are pretty bad for me, too. OK, I'm almost out of time. Let me just tell you what you need to know. I'm going to tell you how to recognize if the thing has malfunctioned, OK, so please listen carefully and remember everything. All you have to do is check the lock. If the dials have reset themselves to 000, or if you can't rotate them on your own and the number keeps going down every fifteen seconds, that means the timer is going. If that happens, you have to get it outside as fast as you possibly can and then just get the hell away, get as far as you possibly can in whatever direction is upwind from the suitcase. You got that?"

Shiori repeated her earlier question. "You're definitely not lying to me?" She mentioned, too, that Tsugumi had warned her he couldn't be trusted an inch.

"I can't believe you're saying that—that you trust her! Listen, what kind of benefit could I possibly derive from calling you like this, on an international line, after all this time, just to trick you? But OK, if you're feeling that skeptical, let me tell you a little about what's going on here, on my end. My bosses over here realized much sooner than I expected that the suitcase I'd brought back was a fake. That and this malfunction with the other suitcase have thrown our organization into a state of chaos. Lots of conflicting motivations with no way to adjudicate among them. So that was bad enough. And then the leaders decided to drive out a bunch of our members, and they all started talking. Not just one or two. Lots of these guys. And that's got me on the run, all alone. I don't know if someone ratted on me or if this whole thing was a set up, but either way I'm in a really bad position. It won't be long before someone from the group turns up on your doorstep, either. So before that happens, you need to take that thing and leave it somewhere where it won't be noticed. Do it as soon as you can—today. It's night there, I guess, but the trains should still be running. If you can't make the trains, take a taxi. Even if the lock happens to start moving, you should still be able to take it somewhere, depending how much time is left. The longest duration until detonation is four hours and ten minutes, right? From your apartment, you could make it to Shibuya in twenty, I'd say. Shibuya. That's it! Take it to Yoyogi Park. Hide it in the bushes. Hide it well, though. Then just forget all this ever happened.

Even if it detonates, it's not your fault. If someone from the group shows up, tell them you don't know anything, just keep repeating that. Don't fool yourself into thinking it will be better to hand it over—I promise you, it won't. When people know, they don't just leave them to go on with their lives, and they'll blow that thing up for sure. I'm sorry, I don't mean to scare you. I know this is all my fault, I'm the one who exposed you to this danger, and I'm sure you must hate me for doing something so awful. It's true, I accept your harshest criticisms. But right now "

Suddenly there was a sharp bang on the other end of the line, followed an instant later by what might have been the sound of the phone itself being smashed. Then silence.

Shiori let her arms fall limply to her sides, dropped her phone on the floor and sat down heavily on her futon. "I'm tired of this," she muttered. She sat with her head down for a while, feverishly pulling at her hair, as if that might relieve the stress.

She would have liked to zone out, but Manuel's marvelously fluent Japanese kept replaying itself in her mind, even as she tried to shut it out, upsetting her more and more.

What should I do? Check the lock, just in case? No, I can't— I'm too scared. And what was this group Manuel belonged to? Would they really come here? Manuel said they wouldn't let me be even if I gave them the suitcase—oh please, I can't take this, I don't even want to think about what that means, what they might do... and this stuff about the malfunction, I mean, should I believe that? With Manuel doing all the talking, I didn't get to ask anything, oh, I'm so scared, I can't take it I can't take it I can't take it, what will I do if Suity malfunctions, too, he said I should avoid electromagnetic radiation... What does that even mean?

Suddenly Shiori felt very cold. She shuddered.

Keep the suitcase away from that kind of radiation, OK? Please.

Electromagnetic radiation. Didn't that include radio waves? Tokyo Tower.

I just got back from Tokyo Tower. And I took the suitcase with me...

Tokyo Tower is a radio tower. Did that make it a place to avoid?

This question instantly drove Shiori's heart rate as high as it had ever been. Her whole body felt ice-cold, and yet she was sweating like crazy, and her palms were so wet she could have been soaking them in a bucket of water.

The only way she could resolve this issue was to go check the lock. And she needed to do that right *now*. She stumbled to her feet and glanced at the clock: 11:06 p.m. She forced herself toward the corner of the room, dragging her feet. Finally, she gathered up the courage to crane her neck and peer at the suitcase, focusing her gaze on the lock.

The three numbers read 460. Had it always said that, or had it gotten there on its own? That was what she needed to know. Figuring this out couldn't have been simpler. All she had to do was watch the dials. If in another fifteen seconds nothing had changed, and it still said 460, she would have no need to regret her trip to Tokyo Tower. But if it said 461...

Just then, she heard a tiny click. Her last hope had been obliterated.

●

Saturday, July 16, 2011, at 11:25 a.m. Shiori was still in her room.

Not because she had succumbed to despair, abandoning whatever courses of action might still be open to her—that wasn't why she remained. She was waiting for Z to respond to an email she had sent, so that she could go out and do something.

The second Shiori realized that the timer on her suitcase had started counting down, she was on it—even before she had time to start thinking, her body had gotten to work. She put on some clothes, began getting ready to go out.

It took only a split second for her to know with absolute surety what she had to do.

Now that the timer had been activated, she had to find some way to get the suitcase out of the city. She had to take it someplace nearby where there weren't any people, and she had to do it alone. Some location where as few people as possible would be exposed to the blast. And she had very little time to get it there. To get *him* there—Suity.

She didn't have all the time in the world, but she did have some. And it was more than just ten minutes or so. According to Manuel's explanation, the number changed every fifteen seconds, so when it flipped to 461 only one hour fifty-five minutes and fifteen seconds had passed. There should be another two and a quarter hours left before it reached 000. Two and a quarter hours from 11:06 p.m... that meant the suitcase would detonate at 1:21 a.m. She should have enough time to move it *somewhere.*

But where?

Shiori had spent the past ten days wandering the metropolis in search of precisely such a location, somewhere she could conceal the suitcase without exposing anyone to danger. And the whole reason she still had it was that her search had been unsuccessful. Leaving the suitcase in any of the places she had visited would have resulted in the loss of countless lives—human, animal and plant—and polluted the entire surrounding area with radiation.

Those parents and children she had seen playing together on the beach at Odaiba Seaside Park, and the couples gazing out at the nightscape from Tokyo Tower... all of them, every last one, would be swept up in the heat of the blast and burned to a crisp, just like the people who suffered such horrors in the bombings of Hiroshima and Nagasaki.

If her apartment in Sangenjaya were ground zero, everyone in that live house, and in the building with the studio, and the convenience store, and the family restaurant, and the park, and the police box... everyone and everything that lived in this area would die.

I can't allow that. I won't. I won't allow myself to commit a crime like that again. I swore to those little birds I killed that I would spend the rest of my life atoning for what I did, and that's what I'll do. I have to fulfill that promise. And now I have this nuclear bomb on my hands, and it's almost time for it to detonate—the only option I have is to take it somewhere where the destruction will be minimized.

But where?

As she landed on that same question, her thoughts fell into a rut. She was starting to feel like she might crack in the face of her inability to answer it, when out of the blue her phone chimed, saving her from that fate. She grabbed her phone. She had an email from Z.

There was something about that incident at Tokyo Tower, he had written, that bothered him. He found it odd that the bearded man had struggled when they took the suitcase from him and returned it to her.

Shiori didn't have the leisure to puzzle over this point, but she was overjoyed that he had chosen this moment to write. Thank you, Z! Thank you! Thank you! she cried. In just a few minutes, she dashed off an email explaining the current situation and sent it to his computer address. She was in such a hurry that the email wasn't as clear as it could have been and it was filled with typos, but Z understood, and this time he wrote back immediately. He didn't seem to think she was making it up, either—he took it seriously. In this email, which had the subject heading "That's really bad," he promised to write back soon, summarizing the information he had gathered when she had first written to ask for his advice and setting out the best options he could come up with.

Shortly after 11:30, two emails from Z arrived. As she skimmed his brief report on nuclear bombs, the first emotions Shiori felt were disappointment and a deep, deep terror.

According to one American movie I watched, if a portable nuclear bomb exploded above ground in the middle of New York, everyone within a five-kilometer radius would be exposed instantly to fatal levels of radiation. About 2,500,000 to 3,000,000 people would die as a result. I know it's a work of fiction, but it seems like a reasonable estimate of what would actually happen. I doubt there's that much of a difference between New York and Tokyo. So, if you're going to leave the bomb where it will do the least possible damage, it seems to me you have to find a location where there aren't any people within at least ten kilometers. Unfortunately, I can't find any such place that you could reach from Sangenjaya within an hour or so. That said, there's no reason to give up yet. I'll write the rest in a separate email.

Still shaking all over from the first email, Shiori opened the second.

I don't want to waste time, so I'll just jump to the conclusion. I can't say whether this is the best possible option, but I think you should get on the subway. Take it to Roppongi Station on the Toei Ōedo line, and get off on track one…

Shiori had read only this far when she stood up, tossed her cell phone and wallet in her tote bag and got out of her apartment as fast as she could, dragging the suitcase behind her.

●

When you get off, you'll be 42 meters below ground. Apparently, that's the deepest station in the city. It's possible the effects of a nuclear explosion would be mitigated if it took place at that kind of depth. I guess it would be like an underground test or something, and if it went well, the blast and the heat might be contained. Of course, I'm not a specialist. At the very least, though, I think you ought to be able to avoid the worst. It's a gamble, but I don't see any alternative. Find an unobtrusive spot on track one of Roppongi Station and leave the suitcase there, hidden. The last train will be long gone by 1:21 a.m., when it's supposed to blow up, so there shouldn't be anyone around. If you're lucky, you might get out alive yourself. All I can do is pray that's the case. I'm sorry. That's the best I can think of, and I can't even help. I feel pathetic being so powerless. It's driving me crazy, actually.

Shiori finished reading Z's email in Sangenjaya Station, on track two, tears streaming down her cheeks. No, she said quietly as she began writing her reply, no, Z—I can't tell you how much you've helped. Your emails have given me the strength to keep going, to keep pushing myself. I'll never be able to thank you enough.

She dragged the suitcase onto the 11:47 p.m. train to Kiyosumi-shirakawa Station on the Den-en-toshi Line. There were a lot of empty seats, but Shiori didn't take one, choosing instead to stand, holding the suitcase against the wall just inside the door. She would have to switch to the Ōedo Line at Aoyama-itchōme, but once she was on that train it would be only another two minutes until she arrived at Roppongi Station.

Shiori had visited Roppongi twice in the past. The first time she went during the day; the second was at night. Both times she had gone with Tsugumi.

An image of Roppongi at night rose up in her mind now, as she leaned against the door. Only the sky was dark: the streets were awash with electric light, so bright it could have been daytime; the major thoroughfares were full of cars, and the side streets, with all their bars and nightclubs and restaurants, were more crowded and livelier than during the day...

Oh no, oh no—Roppongi isn't going to work. We have to find someplace else. So many people would die... Gripped again by panic and terror, Shiori wrote once more to Z to ask for his help. Roppongi was overflowing with people even late at night, she pointed out, and while the explosion would be underground, imagine how terrible the consequences would be if, say, the ground were to collapse.

She got Z's reply just as she pulled into Shibuya. The subject: "You may be right."

I'm sorry, that was careless of me. So, if we have to rule out Roppongi, then the second deepest station is Kokkai-gijidō-mae on the Chiyoda Line. It's 38 meters down. That's the area where the National Diet is, basically it's just a bunch of government buildings, so I doubt there would be anyone around. Either way, sorry to have slowed you down. I hope the connections work out…

The connections worked out. The train Shiori boarded, on the Den-en-toshi Line, arrived at Omotesandō at 11:55 p.m. She carefully made her way down the stairs, holding the suitcase with both hands, and went to track two on the Chiyoda Line. She was able to get on an Abiko-bound train that left exactly at 12:00 a.m. There were more people in the car than she would have expected at that hour, perhaps because it was the last train in the Asase direction.

Shiori reached Kokkai-gijidō-mae just as the clock was about to turn from 12:05 to 12:06. After watching the train she had come on—the last for Abiko until the morning—leave the station on track four, she glanced up and down the platform to get a sense of her surroundings. She couldn't see the whole station because it was subtly curved, and the pillars between the tracks going in either direction blocked her view.

She noticed that a few of the rectangular panels in the ceiling—they seemed to be made of tin or something—were missing. Overall, the tunnel had a dank, depressing, dilapidated air. Shiori began to worry whether a station like this could withstand a nuclear blast without completely collapsing.

No more trains would be coming on track four, but track three was still active. Several passengers stood scattered along the platform, and a steady stream kept walking onto it from the stairs at one end and then going off at the other. All this was very inconvenient for Shiori, who needed desperately to conceal the suitcase, and to do so as soon as possible. The final train on track three was the 12:18 to Yoyogi-Uehara. She would have to be on it if she were going to get out of the station—that meant she had about ten minutes. She needed a hiding place *now*.

Shiori's eye landed on two maps on the wall—one of the station, one of its surroundings. She saw from the first that the Marunouchi Line went through this station, too. Kokkai-gijidō-mae was connected by an underground passage to Tameike-sannō Station. All those people who kept making their way from one end of the platform to the other were headed from the Ginza and Nanboku Lines, which stopped at Tameike-sannō, to the Marunouchi line.

The second map showed that the National Diet and various related institutions, along with the Cabinet Office, the two structures of the Prime Minister's Official Residence, and a host of other buildings were located more or less directly above the Chiyoda and Marunouchi lines. Seeing this made Shiori's expression stiffen, and she gulped down the tiny amount of saliva that remained in her nearly bone-dry mouth. Urgent though the situation was, she still had the presence of mind to grasp that a nuclear explosion in this tunnel could well paralyze the nation, making it impossible for the state to function. Still, there was no longer any possibility of moving to another location, and she figured it was better to let the suitcase explode here, underground at Nagatachō, which would be largely empty at night, than back at Roppongi, where countless ordinary people could end up dead.

Checking the time of the last train on the Marunouchi Line, Shiori discovered that it was the same as the last on the Chiyoda line. She just had to wait until 12:18, and the station would be completely empty. No more passengers. All she needed to do was to put the suitcase in an unobtrusive spot somewhere along the platform—hide it behind something, perhaps—then, after keeping an eye on it until the last moment, jump onto the last train, bound for Yoyogi-Uehara, as the doors were about to close. If she could do that, she would have accomplished her mission. She gripped the suitcase's handle. She was ready. She was going to do it.

She didn't see anywhere on the platform where she could hide a suitcase very well, but she didn't have time to be choosy—everything would fall apart unless she found a spot, even if it wasn't very good. By then, she had made her way to the end of the platform where the stairs led up to the Marunouchi Line. Her eye landed on a white steel drum labeled "Empty Cans & Bottles" that stood between a vending machine and a bank of two public phones. The lid was locked. It was almost 12:09. According to the schedule, the second-to-last Yoyogi-Uehara-bound train would depart from track three in one minute. Shiori decided to push the suitcase between the drum and the phones and then edge away, making like she was planning to board that train. She would try it out, see what happened.

As the train came gliding into the station, Shiori cast a backward glance at the suitcase and darted away. She strode right up to the line behind which passengers were supposed to wait. The doors of the last car opened, and a few people stepped out and rushed up the stairs, probably on their way to catch a Marunouchi Line train. Staring into the now empty car, Shiori began to believe her plan might just work. She made as if she were going to board the train. She wasn't actually planning to pass through the doors, not yet—it was just a test. This little step caused a misunderstanding, however. Feeling a tap on her left shoulder, Shiori spun around to find a middle-aged station attendant, breathless from having sprinted over from who knew where.

"Miss," he sputtered. "Your suitcase! That's yours, right?"

For a moment Shiori considered telling him that he was mistaken, it wasn't hers, but the words wouldn't come. She managed to pretend she hadn't heard him, offering up a puzzled "Sorry? What?" But when he led her over to the suitcase, she admitted it was hers.

The train's conductor, having seen her getting ready to board, called out over the speakers, "The train's about to leave! If you're going to ride, hurry up and get on!"

The station attendant, too, urged her to go, but she said it was all right, she would wait for the next train.

The attendant signaled to the conductor that he could go, and the conductor closed the doors. Gradually increasing its speed as it went, the Yoyogi-Uehara-bound train pulled out of the station and thundered off down the tunnel.

"The next train is the last, so don't miss it. The station shuts down almost immediately after the last train leaves."

The attendant watched Shiori suspiciously out of the corners of his eyes before marching off toward the Tameike-sannō end of the station, inspecting the platform as he went.

Watching him leave, stooping to pick up bits of trash and so on, regarding everything so thoroughly and carefully it almost seemed to be meant for show, Shiori sighed. This wasn't going to work. Already, in her mind, the plan she had just formulated was out.

She sensed the precious seconds passing.

She no longer had time to devise a replacement plan. That didn't alter the fact that within the next seven or eight minutes, she would have to find some place in this station, other than the platform, where she could conceal the suitcase.

The toilet! she thought, and immediately turned back to the station map. It looked as if all the toilets at this end of the platform, near the Marunouchi Line part of the station, were outside the ticket gates. There was one at the other end, though, in the passage that led to Tameike-sannō Station. If she was reading the map right, she would only have to go up one flight of stairs to get there, so it would still be quite deep underground.

Gripping the suitcase's handle, Shiori ran as fast as she could down the platform on the track-four side of the tunnel, heading for the opposite end. She passed the attendant, who was now walking on the track-three side, but she didn't see how he could fault her for hurrying.

A metal plate warning "This Station is Monitored by Camera" hung on a large pillar just outside the entrance to the bathroom. In order to get here, she had ridden the escalator up a level from the Chiyoda Line and hurried down a spacious hall with slick walls, evidently acrylic. After all the trouble she had taken to reach this toilet, this was the sign that met her eye.

Glancing up, she saw that there was indeed a security camera hanging above the door to the toilet. Some distance down the wide, smooth passage, she saw a second black hemisphere stuck to the ceiling. Another camera.

If that attendant, or some other, should happen to be eyeing the monitors now, he would definitely be suspicious when he saw her leave the toilet without the suitcase. And he would come and check the bathroom, and he would find it.

Shiori felt as if she might collapse. Her face was ashen. She teetered on the verge of despair. Not simply because her plan had broken down yet again, no—she wanted to burst into tears and wail at her own stupidity for failing, until it was much, much too late, to give any thought to the station attendants.

Who knew, maybe that guy would be here until the morning? And maybe he wasn't the only one—there could be two nightwatchmen, or more. And if that was the case, she would be willfully abandoning them, knowing they would die. What was she supposed to do? What was she supposed to do? What...

Maybe she should tell him. Confess that the suitcase was a nuclear bomb. But how would she persuade him, now that she had erased Manuel's emails? And persuade him immediately? No one would take a crazy story like this seriously, especially not when they had it sprung on them out of the blue. And if it took until 1:21 to explain the situation, everyone would die. They would all be killed, and she would be to blame.

She had to find some way to communicate to the attendant that a nuclear explosion was imminent. And then make sure the suitcase was left at the deepest place in the station.

There was no time. Not enough. She didn't have the luxury to think. Maybe she just had to summon the courage, steel herself—do it. No, not maybe. This was it.

With tears in her eyes, chewing her lips so hard they bled, she nodded fiercely to herself and, without even taking a look at the bathroom, turned back in the direction she had come from. Once she was back on the Chiyoda Line platform, she hurried down the track-four side, still dragging the suitcase behind her.

She had only one thought. There were no other options.

The clocks on the digital displays read 12:15. In three minutes, the final train would grind in on track three, and, as soon as it left, the station would be closed.

Arriving back at the end of the platform near the stairs to the Marunouchi Line section, she took a quick glance around. Fortunately, there were no other passengers nearby, and she saw no sign of the attendant. Perhaps because this area of the station was older, there were no security cameras hanging from the ceiling or on the pillars between the tracks—at least not that she could see. Maybe she was overlooking them. Either way, she didn't have time to worry about such things. There wasn't a second to waste.

It's now or never. As quietly as she could, Shiori slowly lowered the suitcase down by the rails on the track-four side, where no other trains would be coming. The weight was more than her arms could bear and the handle nearly slipped from her grasp, but she fought desperately to hold on, and she did. She got the suitcase down onto the tunnel floor.

Now it was her turn. She crouched at the edge of the platform with her back to the rails, planted her hands on the lip of the concrete overhang, leaned her upper body forward with her elbows jutting out on either side of her body, and then stuck first one foot and then the other out behind her. Raising her upper body, she was left supporting herself with her arms, her legs hanging out over the tracks. Then, in one motion, she pushed off from the platform with her arms, throwing her legs back. She twisted her right ankle badly as she landed beside the suitcase and couldn't help crying out from the pain. Then she heard the sound of a train, and a moment later the last train came in on track three. Shiori dragged the suitcase onward into the darkness of the tunnel, where no one would see.

●

The searing pain in Shiori's right foot kept her from standing upright, so the only way she could move was by leaning on the concrete wall and scooting forward a bit at a time. She got her phone out of her tote. Worried that the chime announcing an incoming email might alert the station attendant to her location as he patrolled the platforms, she put the phone on silent mode.

At the same time, she discovered that she had two emails. She'd been so shut up within her own consciousness since she arrived at the station that she hadn't even heard the chime. Both emails were from Z. Opening her inbox, she saw the titles: "Did you make it to the station?" and "How's it going?"

The last train for Yoyogi-Uehara pulled out of the station, roaring like a wild beast. As it retreated into the distance, the platform behind Shiori gradually subsided into silence again; there was nothing to be heard but the station attendant's footsteps.

No doubt as soon as he finished his inspection, all the lights in the station would go out. Without the fluorescent bulbs in the tunnel, Shiori would be left in total darkness, unable to tell left from right, up from down. In the past, she would have burst into tears at the thought of the unbearable terror she would feel, the vulnerability. Now that she had steeled her will, focused her mind on the one thing she had to do, she could at least try to remain calm and collected, pushing away her old, fearful, crybaby self.

She checked the time on her phone: 12:20 and a few seconds.

In one hour, the suitcase would explode.

Realizing that she ought to send a last email to Z before her battery ran out, she opened a new message and began busily typing away with her thumbs. She was still writing when the lights on the platform went off, followed by those in the tunnel.

Sorry I couldn't reply sooner. I've hidden the suitcase on the platform at Kokkai-gijidō-mae. I'm just about to get on the last train. I was really scared, but I've calmed down a bit now. I'm sure I'll feel terrible again after the explosion, but it could have been worse. If I'd had to do all this on my own, I'm sure millions of people would have ended up dead. It looks like we've escaped that, and it's all thanks to you. Thank you, Z. You and I have never actually met, or even talked on the phone. Sometime soon I'd like to come see you so I can thank you in person. Actually, I've got just one more request before that, though. Could you get a message to the station attendants and the people who work on the tracks and so on at Kokkai-gijidō-mae, telling them they need to get out because a bomb is going off there at 1:21? I have the sense the attendant will be staying in the station, even after the last train, so it would be great if you could try to call him. I should do it myself, really, but I don't know the number, and my phone is almost out of batteries. Thanks. If possible, please wait a little before you call so they won't find the suitcase. Time it so they'll feel like they need to get out immediately. I appreciate it. Sorry to push this off on you. Well, then—goodbye. Thank you so very, very much.

Sitting in the pitch black, her face illuminated by the screen of her phone, Shiori sent off the email. She prayed he wouldn't realize she had lied to him. A few moments later, he sent a reply. The subject was "That's a relief," while the email itself said simply, "I'll call the station."

It occurred to Shiori that it might be best to go further down the tunnel, just in case the attendant decided to look for the suitcase when Z called. Before standing up, she reached down and gently stroked her right ankle. The area around the bone felt warm and had swollen up as big as a fist. She could hardly bear to touch it again. She felt the pain changing—it was getting numb now, in a hot sort of way, and she had the idea that everything below the shin was puffy. In order to make any progress, she had to put all her weight on her left foot and use the suitcase like a walker.

Pushing the suitcase before her, Shiori limped step by step into the perfect darkness ahead. She could only move a few dozen centimeters at a time, but she kept going even so, grinding her foot into the ground, letting herself be absorbed by the darkness. Gradually she was ceasing to feel the dampness in the air, or the temperature, so it almost seemed as if she were wandering in another dimension. It was silent but for her breathing and the suitcase's rattling wheels.

Five or six meters along, the wheels snagged on something, throwing Shiori off balance. The suitcase took her with it when it capsized, so she ended up sprawled on top of it. As she struggled to right herself, something sharp—a nail or a shard of metal—dug into her blouse, tearing it and cutting deep into her breast. She felt blood streaming down her skin. Her arms and elbows and the palms of her hands seemed to have gotten scratched, too—she groaned from the pain, which was simultaneously throbbing and prickly. Anxious to get her bearings, she struggled through the pain-induced haze settling over her mind to switch on her camera's flash and shine it around her.

Unfortunately, the tiny bulb was too weak to show her anything more than the train tracks and, beyond them, just a few meters away, the tunnel's concrete wall. Wheezing, she tumbled back to the ground. She rested a moment. Then, just in case, she tried shining the light in the other direction, toward the tracks on the other side. Again, the light was too feeble: all she saw was the wall. Everything around her was lost in vague shadow. Peering into that shifting darkness, though, she began to think that maybe, somewhere beyond what she could make out, there would be no wall anymore, and without even particularly intending to she began creeping forward again. Stepping over a track, she turned on the light once more.

Again, a gray wall rose up before her, betraying her hopes. Or so it seemed at first, until she noticed something shining. In the midst of what should have been more of that expanse of bare concrete, something was reflecting the light, if only dimly. She felt a flicker of curiosity.

Drawing on that last reservoir of interest and desire, she stood unsteadily on her left foot. She hopped forward toward the spot where she had seen the gleam, then balanced herself on one leg as she searched for whatever that shiny object was. It didn't take much time to find it or understand why it was there. It was a doorknob. And the doorknob was on a door.

●

The door was iron and looked as if it must have been there for a very long time. It also seemed to be in use, judging from the lack of grime on the doorknob—it was, at least, clean enough to reflect the light.

Whatever it took, Shiori told herself, she was going to get this door open.

It was locked, though, and at first it wouldn't budge at all, no matter whether she pulled or pushed. But she didn't give in—she kept hoping. Maybe, just maybe, she could make it through. Thinking there might be something in the suitcase that she could use to break the knob off, she hopped back to the other side of the tracks and rifled through its contents. She pulled out the clothes and magazines, one after the other, until with some excitement she saw the set of tools. "Yes!" she cried. "Yes!" Once again, she crossed the tracks, and then, illuminating her work with the light from her phone, she set about removing the knob with a Phillips-head screwdriver. She kept stabbing her hand with the point, but ultimately it proved easier than she had imagined. She took off the knob and threw open the door, believing it would lead her out of the tunnel, and this situation.

The door led, however, to another door. This one wasn't locked. She opened it, and found not a hallway or another door, not a ladder that would carry her up, but a small room, about six tatami mats in size, whose purpose she couldn't imagine.

It was a dead end. With this realization, Shiori succumbed to a sudden rush of exhaustion, and she collapsed, both physically and emotionally.

●

After sitting on the floor in a daze for a few minutes, Shiori hauled the suitcase up into the room. She ignored the pain that wracked every part of her body, from all the wounds that afflicted it, using every bit of her strength to move the suitcase to its final resting place.

She took out her phone to check the time: 12:50, going on 12:51. Half an hour until the explosion. Half an hour until this suitcase would go nuclear. What could she possibly do in a mere thirty minutes?...

She had an email from Z. She hadn't noticed when it arrived because her phone was on silent mode. The subject made her start: "Tell me honestly." Opening it, she saw that, yes, Z had intuited the truth. His instincts were amazing.

I've been feeling uneasy since I got your last email, and I can't help writing to ask you this. I want you to tell me the truth. You're still in the station at Kokkai-gijidō-mae, aren't you? Either way, tell me where you are. If you're in the station, you've got to get out of there fast or you're not going to make it. I'm going to call the police. I tried the station office earlier, but no one answered. You may be right that there's a night shift, but if so, he's not picking up. So, I have no choice but to go to the police. Before I do, though, I have to know where you are. Because I have to tell them to save you. Please, tell me the truth. We're out of time.

When she finished reading this email, Shiori beat her head with her fists. Then she sat for a while with her head drooping, considering the situation in which she had found herself, wondering how she ought to reply.

> I'm sorry I made you worry. You're worrying too much, though. I'm still on my way home. Don't be anxious on my account. Please do call the police. I think that's a good idea, just in case. Everyone around the station needs to be evacuated, after all. I'm sure if you tell the police, they can get through to anyone who may be working in the station.

As she sent the email on its way, Shiori muttered to herself that she had lied yet again. She hoped with all her might that Z would believe her. But in the end, he didn't this time, either. He wrote back to say that when he called the police, he would ask them to work with the station attendant to try and find her, because she must be there in the station somewhere. This was the last thing Shiori wanted, so she hurriedly wrote back explaining precisely what her current situation was, hoping this would persuade him not to send the police in after her.

> I'm sorry. This time I'll really tell you the truth. So please don't have them look for me. Please. The thing is, I can't move. I'm physically past my limit, and I can't walk anymore because I broke my right ankle. I had to jump down pretty far. Then I tripped in the dark and cut my chest and my hands and everything, so I've lost a lot of blood. I doubt I'd survive even if I did get out. If people from the station came to help, I'd just slow them down when we tried to escape, and we wouldn't make it out in time. That's the last thing I want. I don't want

anyone else to die trying to help me. I'm sorry I tried to deceive you. I feel terrible, after all the help you've given me, all your kindness. But that was the only option. That was the only way I could think of. I've made up my mind, and I'm OK with this. I've thought a whole lot, a whole lot, about all kinds of things, and I tried my hardest, but this is the most I could do. I think I did pretty well, to tell you the truth. I think it will be OK, thanks to you. So you don't have to feel bad for me. I have no regrets. Thank you. Thank you for everything. I think this is a good time to call the police. I don't want anyone to die.

She had managed to sound brave in the email, but the moment she sent it she began to cry. She sobbed and sobbed. She raised her voice in a wail, releasing such rivers of tears that it seemed there wouldn't be a drop of water left inside her by the time she was done. And yet the tears kept coming. I don't want to die, she said, and it was true. And then, somehow, she was able to cry even more, abandoning herself to her grief.

She came to with a start. Suddenly it occurred to her that she had to hide. She had realized that Z might not do as she asked—he might ask the police to look for her anyway. So she pulled shut both the now knob-less door and the one inside and settled down inside the little room whose purpose was a mystery. The darkness there was even more concentrated than in the tunnel, but her phone's display provided at least a little light. She smiled weakly to herself, feeling like the little match girl in the Andersen story.

"Suity?" she said. But the suitcase refused to speak. Shiori had no idea why he wouldn't say anything, what had made him clam up. But being here in this little room with him, she felt as if she were back in her one-room apartment in Sangenjaya. The darkness was helpful in this respect—being unable to see her surroundings made it easier to feel that way. Maybe if she kept talking to Suity, eventually he would answer? She could imagine his voice: **What is it, Shiori darling?** She wished she could talk to him, even just one back-and-forth, in the time that remained, which was now less than thirty minutes.

Remembering the few CDs in the suitcase, she pulled them out. There were five, three of which happened to be albums Suzuki-kun had played for her in the shed behind his house. She had lent him the money to buy two of those three. She had loved the songs "Mr. Wind" and "Mr. Rainbow." She felt nostalgic thinking back on those days. When she saw the title "Waterloo Sunset," it was as if the song were suddenly being piped into the room, and she started singing the half-remembered lyrics to herself. She hadn't forgotten the prohibition on her singing, but she hoped the little birds up in heaven would overlook it just this once, since she would never have another chance. Quietly, Shiori raised her voice in song.

Come to think of it, Shiori thought when she had finished singing, I never got to say goodbye to Nozomi, or to Mom and Dad. I wish could at least have said goodbye. Nozomi,

I'm sure you'll be mad at me. Mom and Dad, I'm sorry I have to make you so sad. I hope you were able to take care of that issue with the house. I wonder if you found a new place to live. Nozomi, what are you up to these days? I know you're all going through a lot, all three of you, and now I've landed myself in this mess—I'm so sorry I'm doing this to you all, I really am. I should have called my boss, too. I just cause problems for everyone. I wonder if people will think I did it—that I'm the one who set off the bomb. That will make it even worse for Mom and Dad. I'm such a terrible daughter. A terrible, useless daughter. Nozomi, look after them for me—Mom and Dad, and the cats. I'm sorry I was always so weak, that I could never be a good older sister to you. I'm sorry, Nozomi darling...

She was still thinking of her family when a light blinked on her phone, showing that she had an email. She was surprised she could still get email in a place like this.

Z had written to say that he had finally gotten the police to listen. After learning from the station attendant that there actually had been a suspicious woman with a suitcase in Kokkai-gijidō-mae Station, they had immediately gone on high alert.

Learning that everyone working the night shift in all the central subway stations had been ordered to evacuate, Shiori was overcome by a deep, deep sense of relief. Emergency controls had been imposed on traffic in Nagatachō and the surrounding areas, Z explained, making it impossible for anyone to get in. Finally, he told her he wanted her to call him. She had to.

> The police and the station attendant couldn't find you. I was an idiot. If I had just been faster, more engaged, more serious, things wouldn't have ended up like this. It seems like the police should have reached my house by now, but they haven't. We're almost out of time. We're at ten minutes. I want to talk to you. I'll put my number at the end of this message. Please. I can't let you die. Call me.

Not even ten minutes, Shiori murmured to herself. She debated whether or not to call Z. If the police and the station attendant were still on the platform, they might try to take her with them, and then there wouldn't be time to escape. People would die, and it would be her fault. Maybe I should tell him I'm somewhere I can't get out of? Oh, what am I supposed to do?... What should I do?...

Shiori darling, quit fussing. If you want to call him, just do it. Say goodbye to him, at least. You won't be doing anything once the countdown ends. I'd like to help you, you know, but I can't wait.

You're right, Suity, Shiori replied. She would call Z. She highlighted the number at the end of the message and hit call.

She knew the phone should work, since she was getting his emails, but for some reason it was taking an unusually long time for his phone to start ringing. She was so tense she could hardly breathe. When the ringing finally started, it matched the pounding of her heart in her chest, and in her mind both sounds seemed to echo the howl of time itself as the bomb's timer relentlessly chipped away at it. By now the lock must be well past 960, but she didn't know how far—970? 980? 990?—and she was too terrified to look.

The ringing stopped, and she was connected to an answering service.

Something must have happened, and Z couldn't answer. Part of her was relieved at this. She decided to leave a message.

"Hi, this is Shiori. I just called to say thank you. Thanks for being my friend. It makes me so happy, feeling that I'm not all alone. That's enough for me. I mean that. No matter what happens, please don't be sad. I hope you get better soon. I know you will, I know it. I'm sure of it. All right, then—goodbye. I'm sorry I dragged you into all this. I'm glad I was able to tell you how I feel at the end, in my own voice…"

After she hung up, Shiori sat down facing the suitcase. She closed her phone, removing the only source of light, leaving herself in absolute darkness.

It's about time, I guess, she said.

Yeah, we're getting there, said Suity.

OK. Shiori hugged her knees to her chest, cocked her head. She began singing a song—one of her own.

A light started blinking on her phone. She had a call. The display showed Z's number. She wasn't sure she should answer, but she put the thumb of her right hand on the CALL button and began to press it anyway.

Just then, the darkness that had filled the room suddenly slipped away, as if it were peeling from the walls, and Shiori saw bursting from a crack in something in front of her a flood of brilliant white light that radiated outward, spreading in all directions.

Her thumb still resting on the CALL button, she gazed into that glittering, too-bright light, unable to look away, tears flowing from her eyes, and whispered: *Suity*.

With each passing instant, the light from the suitcase increased in brilliance, enveloping Shiori's entire body in a glow as overwhelming as the sun's.

●

Thus, the old man said, Shiori ended her nineteen-year life.

I can't remember how long it took him to tell the entire story. Maybe it was only three or four days; maybe it was two or three weeks. In any event, while I don't think I could ever say there's a fitting length for an account of a person's life, he certainly provided a very detailed and thorough presentation of how that young woman, Shiori, had lived.

When one of us asked the man why he put so much heart into a made-up story, he got very red in the face and told us it wasn't made-up, it had really happened.

Then why was he the only one telling it? Why had he committed himself to this?

At first, he wouldn't say. But in the face of our repeated suggestions that he had invented the whole thing, he finally shared his secret.

●

Half of the responsibility for her death lies with me. If I had only listened to her from the first, believed her, I doubt she would have died. I'm sure there were any number of ways we could have gotten her out of the terrible predicament she was in. And yet, until it was almost too late, until she sent me that email saying, "I'd like to come see you so I can thank you in person," I thought it was all just a game, that we were merely aligning a bunch of fantasies. Yes, I thought all those emails she sent me were just one big fiction, and I thought it was fun, and treated it like a game, trying to come up with solutions to the problems she gave me.

From the time we first started exchanging emails, I had been skeptical of a good portion of what she wrote. Not because anything she wrote felt like a lie, I should say—the problem was on my end. I was sick. I never trusted what people said. I'm still that way, actually—sadly. I'm not as bad as I used to be, but I still don't take statements at face value, not entirely.

Back then, I found it impossible to communicate with people in person. I couldn't do it. The simplest conversation rapidly devolved into a sort of code-breaking. Talking with others was an overload of information. Each tiny thing seemed pregnant with meaning. Changes in expression and tone, gestures—it all interfered with my ability to comprehend their words. I shunned all emotion, no matter who it might be coming from. I was repelled, in fact, by the mere existence of other living people, the verbosity of their bodies. I would have been perfectly happy if they had all been turned into traffic signs. I could have dealt with them then.

When I communicated by email, I was able to let go, to tell myself it was all a chain of mutual dissimulation. It didn't matter whether what you wrote was true or not—in the end, you didn't know your correspondent anyway.

I read her emails, I suppose you could say, like a serialized novel. They helped alleviate the boredom I felt otherwise, having had to take a leave from high school and stay at home all the time. The content always had a subtle air of truth, and that kept me from losing interest. I was a fan, and so I tried to respond to every email she sent me, to keep the novel she was spinning out, one installment after the next, from ending.

So, when she sent me that first email about the suitcase nuke, I regarded it as a new twist in the story. And an unwelcome one. The whole setup was so ludicrously unrealistic that for a while I just stopped replying, because it seemed too ridiculous to play along.

In the end, though, I couldn't give the game up. When I didn't write for a while, I got an email from her saying it turned out the suitcase wasn't really a nuclear bomb, and so I just went on interpreting the situation in my stupid way, assuming she must have realized she had taken the plot in a weird direction and needed to take it somewhere else. So I was kind of stunned when the nuclear bomb thing came back. Stunned, yes, but also curious, this time, to see just how far we could carry the story before it fell apart—and so, like someone working through a list of questions on a quiz program, I decided to play along with her until we couldn't go any further. To make sure I could reply promptly, I did a bunch of research online about nuclear bombs and so on. In other words, I saw the whole thing as a sort of competition in which we would keep writing back and forth until one of us couldn't keep up the pretense any longer and had to surrender. Even as the situation grew progressively starker, even as the options closed down, I was so clueless that I only half believed it all until the end, when I finally reached out to the police. And by then it was too late to save her.

That's what happened. So the responsibility for her death lies with me. More than anyone, I deserve to be punished. And so, though I know full well nothing I can ever do will earn me forgiveness for what I did to her, I hope that by passing on the story of her life, I might at least learn something about how to be with the truth. Here on this spot, after all, that young woman who saved millions of lives lost her own.

That's right: the suitcase exploded here, underground. The buildings and the subways that used to be here were rendered useless as a result, but not a single person died. No one, that is, except for her—no deaths, even though a nuclear bomb exploded here. It all turned out just as she had hoped. She didn't take anyone with her. Not one person. It's unbelievable, isn't it? And she did all that on her own. She made a miracle happen.

Very few people in this country know the story, because it has been kept secret. Everyone who was involved at the time has been ordered to keep silent. The story doesn't appear in any textbooks. That's why you've never heard it before.

No one can stop me from talking, though—not the government, not anyone. This huge wasteland we're standing in is supposed to have ended up this way on account of an earthquake, but of course that's ridiculous. If an earthquake had destroyed the National Diet, they could have built a new one on the same spot. There's a reason they left this place empty. Because the bomb exploded right around here, deep underground. Because her soul rests in this place.

She called me at the very end, just before she died, but I was dealing with the police and couldn't pick up. Until the last, I never once had a chance to speak with her directly. I still have the message she left then, though—I treasure it. Whenever I want, I can listen to her voice. She had a beautiful, beautiful voice. So gorgeous you almost think it can't have been true that she was tone deaf.

On another note, doesn't it strike you as odd that so many people visit this wasteland of a park, day after day? I myself hardly know what to make of it—of the fact that I'm not the only one drawn to this spot. Of course, despite all they've done to keep the blast a secret, rumors have been going around for a long time now. I've been telling the story of the miracle she wrought for quite a while, too. Maybe all these people come here because, through one channel or another, they have brushed up against the truth.

No, there are too many of them for that. They don't all look like they have heard her story. And even assuming they know, and that they come as a way of remembering her, what makes them all look so happy? What brings those smiles to their faces?

One day, listening to the sound of the wind, I understood the reason. Here, I want you all to be quiet. Focus. Do you hear that? The lovely, heartrending sound of a young woman in tears, sobbing as she struggles mightily to endure the terror she feels, not to be crushed, even in the face of an absolutely desperate situation. A sweet, painful song, half crying, not unlike the plaintive chirping of a cage full of lovely little birds...

KAZUSHIGE ABE

PUSHKIN PRESS

NIPPONIA
NIPPON